Readers love
K.C. WELLS

Out of the Shadows

"*Out of the Shadows* is an extremely sweet book about two men who embrace beauty as an extension of love."

—Joyfully Jay

"I recommend this story for a light, feel good romance!"

—The Novel Approach

Before You Break

"Whether you have read Collars and Cuffs or not, this is a wonderful entry book to an enchanting new series."

—Happy Ever After, *USA Today*

"As always with these authors, I couldn't put this story down and I'm still suffering a little from the book hangover it left me with."

—Love Bytes

Step by Step

"Once I started reading I didn't want to stop for even a minute. It was the perfect book for me at the perfect time."

—On Top Down Under

"In the end, I just had a great time reading this, will absolutely put it on my favorites shelf, and I know I'll be back to read it again soon."

—Gay Book Reviews

By K.C. WELLS

With Parker Williams: Before You Break
BFF
Debt
First
Love Lessons Learned
Step by Step
Waiting For You

COLLARS & CUFFS
An Unlocked Heart
Trusting Thomas
With Parker Williams: Someone to Keep Me
A Dance with Domination
With Parker Williams: Damian's Discipline
Make Me Soar
With Parker Williams: Dom of Ages
With Parker Williams: Endings and Beginnings

DREAMSPUN DESIRES
#17 – The Senator's Secret
#40 – Out of the Shadows

LEARNING TO LOVE
Michael & Sean
Evan & Daniel
Josh & Chris
Final Exam

SENSUAL BONDS
A Bond of Three
A Bond of Truth

Published by DREAMSPINNER PRESS
www.dreamspinnerpress.com

BFF

K.C. WELLS

Published by
DREAMSPINNER PRESS

5032 Capital Circle SW, Suite 2, PMB# 279, Tallahassee, FL 32305-7886 USA
www.dreamspinnerpress.com

This is a work of fiction. Names, characters, places, and incidents either are the product of author imagination or are used fictitiously, and any resemblance to actual persons, living or dead, business establishments, events, or locales is entirely coincidental.

BFF
© 2018 K.C. Wells.

Cover Art
© 2018 Reese Dante.
http://www.reesedante.com
Cover content is for illustrative purposes only and any person depicted on the cover is a model.

Trade Paperback ISBN: 978-1-64108-000-2
Mass Market Paperback ISBN: 978-1-64108-124-5
Digital ISBN: 978-1-64080-100-4
Library of Congress Control Number: 2017911490
Published June 2018
v. 1.0

Printed in the United States of America
∞
This paper meets the requirements of
ANSI/NISO Z39.48-1992 (Permanence of Paper).

Acknowledgments

THANK YOU to my betas, Helena, Daniel, Will, Mardee, and Sharon. A huge thank-you to Jason Mitchell, my wonderful alpha—you ROCK. Sharon Simpson—you did it again. Thank you for your technical expertise.

The following article proved invaluable when putting together a Valedictorian speech:

https://brightside.me/inspiration-psychology/25-surprising-psychology-facts-that-will-help-you-better-understand-yourself-and-others-163255

And finally, but by no means least…

Thank you to Mike Iamele, whose blog post, "I'm An Otherwise Straight Man (Who Fell in Love with His Best Friend)" of August 2014, inspired me to write this book. Thank you, Mike and Garrett, for letting me use your real life story as the basis for *BFF*.

(The sweetest part about this? They're getting married.)

https://www.mindbodygreen.com/0-14997/im-an-otherwise-straight-man-who-fell-in-love-with-his-best-friend.html

Prologue

I've ALWAYS wanted to write a novel.

Even when I was a kid, I loved writing. My mom remembers me handing her my first "book" when I was five or six. I'd taken several pages from a drawing book, written God knows what on them, and then folded them over. Of course, my writing was for shit back then, but apparently I was so proud of myself. I'd even drawn a pretty picture on the cover.

So yeah, I guess the idea stuck with me, although it got shoved to the back burner for a while. Grandpa had a hand in that. He agreed with me that, yes, most people had a book in them somewhere. His view, however, was that for some folks, it should definitely stay there.

When life threw me a curve ball, it made me look at myself in a whole new way. Nothing like staring death in the face to make you reevaluate your existence. So when Matt brought up the topic of NaNoWriMo, I figured it was fate giving me a shove in the right direction. Get that book out of my system once and for all.

For those of you not in the know, NaNoWriMo is National Novel Writing Month, and it happens every November. The goal is to write fifty thousand words in thirty days. When Matt first mentioned it, I'll be honest: I stared at him and said, "Are you fucking *crazy*? 50K? Yeah, right." Then, when I'd stopped laughing, he tried to put it to me another way. He went on his phone, pulled up his calculator app, and said if I broke it down, that was 1.6K a day. Sixteen hundred words, people! That made a difference. That was a nice, manageable chunk.

Yeah, I could do this.

Only thing was, Matt had to go and ask me a sort of important question: "What are you going to write about?"

Like I had a clue.

I sat around for weeks, tossing ideas back and forth. Matt suggested sci-fi, seeing as I was a die-hard fan of *Star Trek*, *Babylon 5*, *Star Wars*,

Dune, Doctor Who, Torchwood, Battlestar Galactica…. You name it, I tuned in. Great idea, but scary as hell. I mean, we're talking building *worlds* here, and as much as I loved the idea of being the next Isaac Asimov, Arthur C. Clarke, or Frank Herbert, I didn't think I had it in me. Hell, let's be realistic here! So we scratched that one off the list and got our thinking caps back on.

Historical stories put me to sleep. Thrillers? Yeah, think I'll leave those to John Grisham and James Patterson. Fantasy? Sorry, but J.K. Rowling pretty much gets the prize for that one, and if I couldn't write the next Harry Potter, what was the point?

So one night we were sitting quietly after dinner. Nothing on TV to make it worth switching on. Both of us kinda contemplative. Then Matt looked at me, and I swear I saw a light bulb go on behind his eyes.

"Write what you know."

"Huh?"

"Something I read online today. It was a forum on writing, and that was one of the suggestions. If you write what you know, what you're familiar with, it makes things easier. You can draw on your own experiences, and that will make your writing better."

It made sense, I suppose. I considered the idea. "Okay. So what could I write about?"

He gave me one of those smiles of his that lights up the room. "Us. Write about us."

"Why would people wanna read about us? And would I have enough to write about?"

Matt laughed. "Are you kidding? How old were we when we first met? Seven?"

"I guess."

Matt was nodding, his eyes bright. "That means we've been friends for twenty years, David. Twenty years. Face it, you could write a book based on the last couple of years alone and you'd have a damn sight more than 50K."

He had a point. They sure had been… eventful. "When you put it like that…."

Matt grinned. "See? What did I tell you? Pulitzer Prize winner, right there."

It was my turn to laugh. "Not sure about that part, but…." I had to admit, it was a great idea. There was just one thing. "Where in the hell would I start it?"

Matt was giving me That Smile again. "At the beginning, where else?"

I could see it now.

Once upon a time, there were these two little boys sitting next to each other in class….

Chapter One

1996, Van Hise Elementary School, Madison, WI.

MRS. DELANEY handed me back my test, and I beamed when I saw the gold star.

All right!

"Well done, David." She smiled at me. "You're still at the top of the class chart for spelling."

I thanked her and gave Wendy Taylor a sideways glance. Yeah, she looked mad, not that I was surprised. She'd been telling me all week that *she* was going to be top. *Guess it sucks to be her, then.* But soon I pushed mean old Wendy from my thoughts. Mom and Dad were going to be so pleased. Dad had promised that if I got another gold star, that weekend we'd go to the lake. I loved going to Lake Mendota, especially when Dad hired a boat and took us out on the water.

Mrs. Delaney was moving around the classroom, handing back papers and comments with equal measure. The weekly spelling test took place every Monday, and with our results on Tuesday came the slip of paper with twenty more words for the following week's test.

I guess I was lucky. Spelling was never a chore for me, and my favorite subject was English. Listening to Mrs. Delaney read aloud in her quiet voice that still managed to carry around the room was perhaps the highlight of my week. Writing came a close second. Man, I loved writing stories. There were times when I was in my room, sitting on my bed, a pad of paper balanced on my knees and me lost in my writing. Every time I wrote a new story, Mom would listen to me as I read it aloud. Then she'd get me to think about what I'd written.

I'd always remember the time we discussed one of my stories. I'd described this boy, Billy, as being angry.

Mom looked at me for a minute in silence. "David, have you ever seen me really angry?"

I giggled. "Sure. When the mailman brought you a package that was all busted open."

She nodded. "And how did I look?"

I thought for a moment. "Your face was all red and scrunched up, and your nostrils did this funny thing."

"They flared? Like they opened up wide?"

I smiled. "Yeah. That's it."

"Okay, then." Mom pointed to my page. "Well, instead of *telling* me Billy was angry, why don't you *show* me how angry he was?"

I frowned. "But... how do I do that?"

Mom beamed. "You just did it. Write how his face was red, how his nostrils flared. I don't need to see the word 'angry' to know that he is. Your description does that." She sat back in her armchair. "So next time you write a story, think. Is there a way you can describe what your character does or how they look that gives away how they're feeling? Your writing will be better that way."

"I like that. Mrs. Delaney is always telling us to describe things."

Her eyes shone. "There you go. You try it next time you have a story to write, and see what Mrs. Delaney says."

I guess that was the start of my love of writing stories, because after that? Yeah, Mrs. Delaney *loved* my writing.

I have a really cool mom.

And yeah, although English was never that difficult for me, there were other kids who weren't as lucky. Like Matt Thompson, the kid whose family had just moved to Madison and who was now in my second-grade class. Matt sat at the desk next to mine, and I watched him wince every time Mrs. Delaney handed him back a test paper. He usually didn't do so well on tests.

That morning was no different. I glanced across at him, noting how his head was bowed and his hands had clenched into fists. Yeah, Matt was all kinds of miserable.

I took a quick look at Mrs. Delaney, but she was still handing back papers. I leaned across the aisle and whispered, "You okay?"

Matt raised his head and peered at me. "'M fine," he murmured.

He sure didn't *look* fine, but the way he said it sort of made it obvious he didn't want to talk about it. Besides, by then Mrs. Delaney was standing at the front of the class, telling us to make sure we didn't go home without the list for the following week's test. I knew she'd remind us again before we left at the end of the day.

When the bell for recess sounded, I bolted from my chair and made a dash for the door, eager to be out in the sunshine. June had started warm, and I was praying it stayed that way. Only a few weeks to go until the summer vacation started, and I couldn't wait.

"'Snot fair," Wendy whined as I passed her, heading out to the far corner of the yard. "You *always* get gold stars. Just like you do in every subject. It's *so* unfair."

I ignored her. Like I didn't hear the same thing every week. I went on my way, past the group of girls who were jumping rope and the group of seven or eight kids playing tag. I didn't want to play, not that they'd have asked me anyhow. I wanted to find my quiet place by the old tree and sit with my notebook and a pen.

Only when I got there, my usual space was already taken.

Matt sat on the cool grass in the shade of the tree, his back against the wide trunk. His eyes were red, his face puffy, and he was sniffing and wiping at his nose. The sight of him took away my annoyance at finding him there.

"Hey," I said cautiously. "Can I sit with you?"

Matt jerked his head up and stared at me. "Sure." He scrambled to his feet. "I'll leave you alone."

"Hey, no, you can stay." I felt awful, as if my turning up had made him feel even worse than he evidently did.

Matt regarded me, his mouth downturned, his eyes kind of… empty. "Okay," he said carefully, resuming his position. I sat cross-legged on the grass facing him and threw my notepad onto the ground beside me. He studied me for a second or two. "You're David, right?"

I nodded. "Where did you move from?" He'd only joined the class about a month previous.

"Kentucky. My daddy got a new job working for a company that rents out equipment. He's a mechanic."

I liked the way Matt's voice sounded kinda like music when he spoke.

"Cool. Does your mom work?"

Matt shook his head. "She stays home and looks after my baby sister. My brother is in ninth grade." He cocked his head. "What about you? Got any brothers or sisters?"

"Nope, there's just me." I'd always wanted a brother or sister, but so far there had been no sign. I'd resigned myself to it being just me.

Matt nodded and then fell silent, his shoulders hunched over.

Yeah, if he was fine like he said, my name was Mickey Mouse.

I could've kept my mouth shut. I could've... but I didn't. "Wanna tell me what's wrong?"

Matt blinked. "Nothing's wrong."

I huffed. "Yeah, right. Ever since you got your test back, you've looked like you lost a dollar and found a nickel. Didn't you do so well?"

He sighed. "I never do well. I'm... stupid."

It was my turn to blink. "No, you're not."

Matt opened his eyes wide. "Oh yeah? And what would *you* know? Did you see my test paper this morning? My spelling is crap."

"That doesn't mean you're stupid. Besides, I heard you last week when you gave that report about animals in danger of being wiped out. You knew tons about it."

A faint smile crept across Matt's face. "You liked that?"

"Sure!" I hadn't missed a word of it. "You didn't even read it. You just opened your mouth and out it came. Now, that doesn't sound like you're stupid."

He shrugged. "I watched a lot of shows on TV. Plus, my momma found lots of National Geographic magazines, and we talked about it. And I didn't read it because... I don't read so well."

"But that doesn't make you stupid," I protested. "My cousin Donna couldn't read well, but she's as smart as a whip. She's in college now. Turns out she has this thing where she sees words differently." The term escaped me, which irritated me greatly, because words were important.

"Really?"

I nodded. "Her mom and dad got her tested. Then they got her a tutor."

"And... that helped?" Matt bit his lip, his eyes wide and shining.

"Seems so. Hey, maybe you need to get tested too!" I considered the issue. "Do you read at home with your parents?"

7

Matt shook his head. "Daddy doesn't have time. When he gets home from work, he's usually tired, and on the weekend, he does stuff around the house. Momma… she doesn't read so well either." He gazed at me with interest. "Do you read to your parents?"

"To my mom, yeah. We read together every night before I go to bed, and she always helps me when I'm studying for a test."

"Sounds neat." There was an expression of longing on Matt's face.

"Maybe your parents need to ask school for you to be tested like my cousin. Maybe all you need is a little help." Then it came to me. "*I* could help you."

He frowned. "How?"

"Well, I could read with you. Maybe we could get together on the weekend, or after school. My mom wouldn't mind if you came to the house. She'd probably be really happy about it, come to think of it."

"Why's that?"

I waved a hand in the air. "Oh, she's always asking why I never bring friends home from school, or why I never hang out with them." I grinned. "I can't really tell her most of the kids in my class would be happy talking about playing in the sand pit."

Matt snorted.

"Tell you what. Why don't we start today?"

Matt regarded me keenly. "With what?"

"Well, we have another twenty words to learn for next Monday. We could start with them."

Matt arched one eyebrow. "I can't see us making that much of a difference in a week."

"We're never gonna know until we try," I announced firmly. I really liked the idea.

Matt pursed his lips and fell silent. "Okay," he said at last. "Let's give it a try."

"Excellent. You can go home first, if you like, and then come over later. Where do you live?"

"On South Segoe Road."

I gaped at him. "You're kidding. Me too. What number?"

"Four sixty-five."

I beamed. "I'm at one twenty-five. We're neighbors. You have to pass my house on your way to school."

"Neat." Matt's expression brightened. "I'll go home after school and tell Momma. Then I'll come by your house. You're sure your mom won't mind?"

"Positive." I knew she'd be fine with it, and actually? I was looking forward to it. I had a really good feeling about Matt.

Maybe I've finally got myself a friend.

NOTE

JUST READING back through this part and a couple things struck me.

First, there was that whole smart-as-a-whip thing. Okay, so maybe I didn't actually say "smart as a whip." I mean, seriously, what eight-year-old does that? But I did like how it made me sound smarter.

Which brought me to my second point.

That last line…. What prompted that thought? What was it about Matt that made me latch on to him the way I had? I had to sit for a while and think back to that time. What I came up with? I didn't need words to make me sound smarter—I *was* smarter. I don't mean to sound arrogant, but yeah, I was a bright kid. And therein lay the reason why I had so few friends. I was always top of the class, and it turned a lot of them off from wanting me for a friend. Only I *totally* didn't see it back then. I was oblivious to the whole thing. I had no clue why the other kids were so mean to me. I just accepted that it was the way things were in David Lennon's world.

So when Matt walked into it, a kid who needed my help, who didn't resent me because I had something between my ears…. Yeah, you can bet I wanted him for a friend.

Chapter Two

July, 1997

"I'M PRETTY sure we shouldn't be doing this."

It had to be the third time Matt had said it since we told our parents we were going to play soccer before lunch, as we all exited the Covenant Presbyterian Church after the service. Mom had smiled and delivered her usual "Don't be late for lunch" warning, swiftly followed by "And don't get your church clothes dirty," with added eye roll for good measure. Matt's mom had just shrugged and said fine. It wasn't like she didn't care; she just seemed preoccupied. His dad was the same. Darren, Matt's brother, hadn't even bothered to sit with us. He was too busy talking with a girl from his tenth-grade class.

The pair of us had made a run for it before Mom could change her mind and tell me to get changed first.

"I keep telling you, it'll be fine. And besides, can you picture the look on their faces when we come home with a turtle?" It was all I'd thought about for weeks. I'd first had the idea when I'd found a book in the school library all about the painted turtles of Wisconsin. Well, that did it. I was going to find me a turtle.

And Matt was going to help me.

"Do you have a clue where you're going?" Matt sounded less worried and more amused.

"Of course I do," I replied confidently. "I checked on the route last night. We walk up South Segoe until it becomes North Segoe, and then we keep walking until we reach University Avenue." I pulled the folded sheet of paper from my pants pocket and consulted it. "Then we turn left toward Horizon High School, then right, through Indian Hills Park, heading for Merrill Springs Road, and finally Lake Mendota Drive." That would bring us close to the lake.

Matt shook his head, chuckling. "And what makes you think we're gonna find a turtle, just like that?"

I stopped in the middle of the sidewalk. "You don't *have* to come with me, y'know. You can turn around and go home." Of course I didn't mean a word of it, and I was silently praying Matt wouldn't take me seriously. I was banking on him being the best friend I thought he was.

Matt merely arched his eyebrows and did an eye roll. "Like I'm gonna do that." He pointed ahead of us. "Keep going, Christopher Columbus."

I liked that.

Then *he* stopped. "Wait a minute. Do you have any idea how long it's gonna take us to walk that far? Do you even know how far it is?"

Damn. I was hoping he wasn't going to ask that.

"A couple of miles," I muttered under my breath. Okay, so it was closer to three, but he didn't have to know that.

Matt opened his eyes wide. "A couple of *miles*?"

"Look, do you want to help me find a turtle or don't you?" Yeah, I knew it was crazy, two eight-year-old boys on a quest to find a turtle, both of them decked out in their Sunday best.

Total madness.

Matt stood still for a moment, and then he grinned. "You are loony tunes, do you know that?"

The knot in my belly dissolved a little. Matt was still coming with me.

We walked along, the sun beating down on us. Summer vacation had begun a little more than a week ago, and we'd spent that week in each other's company. Granted, Matt still had to see his tutor twice a week, but the rest of the time was ours. My mom joked that she sometimes felt like she'd adopted him, he spent so much time at our house.

"So where are you gonna put this turtle? That's supposing you actually manage to find one."

I glared at him. "Hey. Think positive. We're gonna find one, okay? And how should I know where I'll put it?" I clearly hadn't considered that far ahead. Then I grinned. "How do you think my mom would feel if she found a turtle in the bath?"

Matt dissolved into giggles. "I think you might find yourself grounded. Lord knows how *my* momma would react." He went quiet for a second. "Do you think she might get up onto a chair and scream, you know, like in the Tom and Jerry cartoons?"

I guffawed. "Mice move a lot faster 'n turtles. Why would anyone be scared of a turtle?" Then I reconsidered. Mom had a habit of surprising me. "And who was that girl Darren was talking to after church? She looked kinda familiar."

Matt huffed. "Her name's Melissa, and she has this laugh that goes right through me. You know, like Lawrence Dunn's?"

I shuddered. When Lawrence laughed, you'd have sworn there was a donkey somewhere close by. "Okay, well, apart from her laugh. Is she all right?"

"I suppose. Darren's been seeing her for a couple of weeks." Then Matt chuckled. "Momma was real mad at him yesterday, 'cause Melissa came over, and he wanted to take her into his room. When Momma said no, Darren got all moody, saying how he was fifteen now and didn't she trust him? That was when Momma blew up. She took him into the yard, and she was telling him how he knew better than to ask, and did Melissa's parents let him go into her room when he went over there? Darren said no, and Momma just folded her arms and nodded."

"Wait a minute. How do you know all this?"

Matt grinned. "I was in my bedroom at the time, and my window was open. Anyhow, Darren got into a snit, and he said he was taking Melissa home. After he'd left, Momma and Daddy were talking quietly." He shrugged. "I think girls are more trouble than they're worth. All the girls I know are just plain annoying. Why would you want to be friends with someone like that?"

It beat me too.

"Is everything okay with your parents?" I asked as South Segoe became North Segoe. "They seemed to have a lot on their minds this morning."

Matt sighed. "I'm not sure. They've been doing an awful lot of talking lately. I was scared for a while back there that maybe they were, you know…."

"What?"

"Thinking about getting a divorce." The words came out in a whisper, almost as if he was too afraid to speak any louder for fear of them coming true. "But Darren told me I was just being stupid and that they're fine, so I guess that wasn't it." Matt shuddered. "Good, because that would be too awful for words."

I knew what he meant. Sarah Bannerman's parents were getting a divorce, and Sarah never seemed to stop crying. "So if it's not a divorce…." The skin around Matt's mouth tightened. Maybe it was time to change the subject. "Where are you all going on vacation?" Mom had informed me we were going to spend a week at my grandparents' house in North Carolina. I liked it there. The mountains were just beautiful.

"We're not." Matt's breathing hitched.

"Not going on vacation?" I glanced at him. Matt looked plain miserable all of a sudden. "Hey, don't think about it. We can find all kinds of fun things to do together, I'm sure."

Matt huffed out a breath. "All Momma said was that we couldn't afford it this year and that we had to 'tighten our belts.' I was gonna ask what she meant, but then Daddy told her to hush, and that was the end of the conversation." He stared at our surroundings. "Hey, look at those kids over there."

It felt like he'd deliberately brought an end to the conversation, and I got the message. Matt did not want to discuss this any further.

To our left was a huge parking lot. Usually it was full, but being Sunday, it was empty, and a group of seven or eight boys had set up a couple of ramps and were skateboarding all over the place. They seemed like maybe they were Darren's age. I watched as one boy zipped along, aiming for a steep ramp, but at the last minute, he veered off. His friends started flapping their arms and making chicken noises. Matt was chuckling, and I hissed at him.

"Shh. We don't want them to notice us, all right?" When he gave me a blank stare, I rolled my eyes. "How do Darren and his friends treat you when they're all hanging out together?"

His eyes widened, and I knew he'd gotten it. Older boys could be real assholes.

We walked along, the traffic beginning to pick up beside us, getting noisier. Ahead was a busy intersection, and we stopped at the curb.

"Hey, we're at University Avenue." Matt gave me a half smile. "Maybe if we talk less, we'll walk faster. After all, we've got a turtle to catch." He cocked his head. "Maybe we should have brought something to feed them with, you know, like bait."

"Like what?" I might have been reading up on turtles, but I had no idea what to bring to tempt a turtle.

Matt scratched his head. "Candy?"

I burst into giggles. "I'm pretty sure they don't eat candy."

"There you are," he said triumphantly. "We give 'em candy, and they'll be following us home."

I had to smile at the image in my mind: me and Matt, walking along South Segoe, a couple of turtles trotting behind us. Except turtles don't trot, of course. The more I thought about it, the more decided I became. I was *not* going home without a turtle.

"I sure am glad school's out, though," Matt said a couple minutes later.

"Ugh, me too." It seemed as if I'd spent the last five or six weeks with my eyes glued to the calendar on the kitchen wall. Not that I didn't like school—I was just impatient for summer to really get going. I didn't count June as summer, not when I spent most of it in a classroom. No, summer was what happened when there were no more school bells for several long sunny weeks. Matt and I had made lots of plans. We were going to build a castle in my backyard. Okay, so it would be made of boxes and whatever else we could lay our hands on, but it was going to look like a castle. Mom had mentioned our two families going on a camping weekend together at the lake. Apparently she and Dad had been discussing it with Matt's parents, but I wasn't allowed to say anything until they definitely gave it the go-ahead.

That was fine by me. I wanted to see the expression of total surprise on his face when they told him. He was gonna flip out.

"You know, I can still picture Deke Fletcher's face when we won the science prize." Deke had gaped at us, jaw dropped, eyes bugging out. He'd made a maze, and then he'd put his pet mouse, Daisy, in it at one end and let her run around it to locate the cheese he'd placed at the other end. He timed how long it took her and wrote it down on a chart. Then he did the same thing again and again, only he kept moving the cheese. I thought it was plain mean. Poor little Daisy.

That final Friday morning, he'd carried the maze into the third-grade classroom, beaming and strutting, his chest all puffed out. Yeah, he obviously thought he had the winning project right there. The look on his face when he caught sight of the volcanic island Matt and I had made told me he'd just realized he had some serious competition. The volcano towered over the little island, and we'd made it so that a side of it could be removed to show the magma inside. Except it wasn't *real* magma, but oatmeal that we'd colored with red food dye. It had taken us weeks, involving a lot of time in my dad's garage with newspaper, water, and glue, to get the shape of the island right. Matt had drawn it out first, and his mom put all his sketches together and made them into a notebook. We had pictures of real live volcanoes, magma flows, and those dense clouds of dust and ash that had probably killed all the people in Pompeii.

When Miss Prince read out mine and Matt's name, we high-fived, both of us grinning like idiots. And when the principal, Mrs. Travis, asked if she could put the island in the glass cabinet where they kept the school trophies and cups and press clippings, we were so proud and stunned that neither of us could get a word out. I'd just nodded, and Matt's smile was so wide, his face must have ached.

Matt snorted. "Serves him right. He was so full of himself the last few weeks."

I knew there was more to Matt's reaction than he was telling. "He's been teasing you, hasn't he?"

Matt's startled hiccup was answer enough. "How... how did you know about that?"

I kept my eyes on the road ahead. "I overheard him in the cafeteria. He was bragging to Dylan Levon and Pete Myres about how he 'put you in your place,' as he told it. Something about your tutoring?" That was the scaled-down version of what I'd heard. Matt didn't need to know the rest. God, some kids could be vicious.

"Yeah." The flat tone of Matt's voice told me plenty.

"Well, don't you worry. One, so what if you have a tutor for your dyslexia? He's helping, isn't he? You read so much better than you did a year ago."

"I'm not sure how much progress is because of my tutor, or you, reading with me every day after school." Matt chuckled. "Maybe my folks should pay you instead of Johnny."

I laughed. "No argument from me. I could do with a raise in my allowance."

Matt laughed right along with me. Then he stopped. "Wait a moment. You said, one. That kinda implies there's at least a two to follow it." He paused. "Well? 'Don't you worry,' you said. Keep going."

Crap. "I... might have told Deke to leave you alone."

A sudden silence fell so heavily that I had to stop and turn toward him.

Matt stood there, rooted to the spot, his cheeks pale, squinting in the bright sunlight. "You told him? What exactly did you tell him? And when was this?"

Something about the way he was looking at me made my stomach churn.

"About... about a week before vacation began."

Matt's eyes widened. "Did you... was it you who hit him?"

"I didn't hit him!" I flung back at him. "My dad is always telling me, fists don't solve anything."

Matt arched one eyebrow, the way he did with his expression that said *Oh really?* "Mm-hmm. Then what gave him that bruise on his cheek, if it wasn't one of your fists?" His gaze grew thoughtful. "He wouldn't tell anyone what had happened." He started walking again.

That didn't surprise me in the slightest. I sighed. "Okay. I found him in the boy's bathroom. I told him to leave you alone. When he told me to—" I glanced around and lowered my voice. "—fuck off, I lost my temper and told him that if he didn't back off, I was gonna tell everyone what he was doing in the bathroom."

Matt's eyes were huge. "He said... that?"

I nodded.

"And what *was* he doing?"

"Looking at a magazine full of pictures of girls... who had no clothes on."

Matt whistled. "Really?" He paused. "What was it like?"

I shrugged. "How do I know? I only caught a quick look at one page as I came into the bathroom. But that and the cover were enough."

"That doesn't explain how Deke ended up with a bruise."

"Well, that happened because he came at me, slipped on the wet floor, and banged his face against the sink."

Matt stared at me for a minute and then bit back a smile. "I shouldn't laugh."

"No, we shouldn't," I agreed. Seconds later both of us were laughing our asses off. When we'd regained our composure, I felt the need to ask a question. "So, are we good?"

Matt shook his head and crossed his arms. "No, we aren't. You don't need to stand up to anyone for me. I can do that myself." He stuck out his chin.

"I know you can," I said earnestly, "but you weren't there, and I didn't want him to think he could get away with it. He had to know. If anyone says something to hurt my best friend, I'm not gonna take it lying down." I clenched my teeth.

Matt grinned, his eyes sparkling. "Your best friend, huh?"

I rolled my eyes. "Well, duh. Who else would I have as my best friend? Wendy?"

Matt guffawed. "Good point." We carried on walking, the sun beating down even more strongly. By the time we reached the lake, I'd need to dip my head in it, just to cool off. Not that I'd be venturing out too far. Unlike Matt, I hadn't managed to perfect the art of swimming yet, despite the best intentions of Mr. Hinton, the swim teacher from the Y.

I was going to stick to wading through the water's edge, hoping a turtle would cross my path. I mean, it could happen, right? And I definitely would not be thinking about the fact that we were already late for lunch. Mom would understand when she saw the turtle.

I hoped.

"ANY SIGN?" I called out to Matt, who was farther along the shore, peering at rocks and into pools. I was doing the same, my pants rolled up to my knees, my jacket, shoes, and socks safely out of the reach of the water, lying on the ground beneath the trees that lined the lake.

"Nope, nothing."

I was starting to worry. I had no idea what time it was, but the uneasy feeling in my belly, which might have been hunger but was more likely to have been fear of what Mom was going to say, blossomed into something much bigger. Never mind my previous thoughts that Mom would understand.

Mom was going to be pissed.

"Hey… wait."

I jerked my head up to find Matt pointing excitedly to a boulder a few feet away from me. "There's a turtle sunning itself on this rock." He kept his voice to an agonized whisper.

Finally! I launched myself through water that came halfway up my calves, perilously close to my pants.

"Slow down, you'll scare it off!" Matt was staring at me, his eyes wide.

But it's a turtle! I wanted to yell. I strode toward it, my feet alternately slipping on the algae-covered rocks under the water or squelching in the soft mud that lay between them. I watched, horrified, as I got closer and the turtle poked its head out and began to crawl toward the water.

"No!" I screamed and dove forward, waving my arms, as if that would surely stop the turtle in its tracks and make it wait for me to catch it.

Okay, so I was dumb sometimes.

My arms flailing like some demented windmill, I lurched through the water, lost my footing, and fell face-first into it. Man, it was cold. Thankfully, my face missed the rocks. Unfortunately, my clothes didn't miss the mud. I struggled to my feet and stood there, my clothes soaked and my ego bruised.

Matt guardedly waded across to me, and I could tell he was doing his best not to laugh. "You okay?"

I glared at him. "Well, do I look okay?"

That did it. He burst into a peal of bright laughter that sent all the birds in the nearby trees rising into the air with much flapping of wings. I took a glance at the rock. Yeah, no turtle. I trudged to the edge of the lake and clambered out onto the grass. Matt followed, making sympathetic noises interspersed with giggles.

It was a good thing we were best friends; that's all I could say.

Then it began, the gnawing in my belly that said we'd been an awful long time getting there and heaven knew how long looking for the blasted turtles. I got that sinking feeling that we were going to be in real trouble.

"We'd better head home," I said quietly.

Matt sobered instantly. "Oh. Yeah." We picked up our shoes and jackets and headed back through the trees toward Lake Mendota Drive. Matt glanced at a sign as we reached the road, and his eyes widened. "Hey, did you see this?"

I peered at the sign, reading aloud. "Wally Bauman and Tent Colony Woods. What about it?"

Matt gave me a panicked look. "Maybe we shouldn't have been in there. Someone could've seen us and—"

"But no one did," I reminded him. "So quit worrying. We're gonna go home. My clothes will have dried off by the time we get there, so Mom will never know—"

"David Stephen Lennon, you get over here right this minute, mister!"

I froze. Our car was a few feet away, my mom leaning out of the open window. Shit. She looked mad. I knew better than to tangle with Mom when she was in a snit, so I hurried over the grass toward the car, Matt keeping up with me.

Mom looked me up and down, her eyes bulging. "What have you done to your clothes? For God's sake, you're soaking wet. Get out of those clothes right now. You'll catch your death."

I wanted to tell her that they'd dry off pretty quickly in the heat, but one glance at her expression told me to keep my mouth shut. "Yes, ma'am." I stood beside the car, squirming out of wet pants and a shirt that clung to my body. Mom held out her hands for the soggy items and then put them in the back of the car.

"Matt, you can get in the front. David, in the back."

We weren't about to waste time arguing. I climbed onto the seat and fastened the seat belt across my chest, shivering a little.

"Mrs. Lennon, how did you know where we were?" Matt voiced the question I'd been too scared to ask.

Mom huffed as she drove through the streets. "It wasn't until I looked in David's room and saw his books open that I realized what you two were up to. Turtle hunting, hmm? I figured you'd head for the lake. I've been driving up and down this road for the past half hour, trying to catch sight of you. Two hours! You've been gone for two hours! I was going crazy, thinking that something had happened to you." She glanced over her shoulder at me. "And if you think I'm going to be letting you out of the house anytime soon, you can think—"

"It was my fault," Matt blurted out.

I stilled. What?

Mom gave him a smile. "Matt, I know you two are friends, but—"

"No, really. We were playing around in the water, and I… I pushed him. It's my fault he ended up in the lake, ma'am. Honestly."

I couldn't believe what I was hearing. Not that I could let him do that, though. "Matt, it's—"

He twisted around and glared at me. "I'm sorry I pushed you. And I should never have put the idea in your mind about finding a turtle." I could almost read the words he was holding back in his eyes. *Play along.*

Mom said nothing for a moment. Finally she sighed as she pulled into our driveway.

Ten minutes. It had taken us all that time to get there, and she'd brought us home in ten lousy minutes. Somehow that made it seem less of an adventure.

She switched off the engine and turned to look at us both. "What am I to do with you two, hmm? I suppose boys will get up to this sort of thing."

"And I promise we won't do anything like this ever again," Matt said earnestly, his gaze locked on hers. "I mean, if you still think you need to ground David, then—"

Mom smiled. "By the look of him, David's had enough punishment for one day. But you two need to promise me you won't go off again without telling us where you're going." She peered at Matt. "I imagine your mom will have a few words to say to you when you get home."

"Yes, ma'am." Matt's shoulders sagged, his tone glum.

"Then you'd best get off home. I'll call her, though, to tell her how you spoke up and told the truth. Maybe she won't go so hard on you." Her gaze met mine. "And you need to get into the house and have a bath."

"A bath?" Well, that sure sounded like punishment.

Mom's eyes suddenly had steel in them. "You fell into the lake. Heaven knows what you might have picked up in that water. So you will have a bath. No arguments."

I sighed. "No, ma'am."

See, I really did know when to keep my mouth shut.

NOTE

OF COURSE, that was when Matt decided it was time he taught me to swim. God knows why he thought he'd have more success than the swimming teacher, but he was determined.

I'll always remember the day we hunted for turtles. Matt didn't need to do that, but he did it anyway, to save me from the trouble he knew was coming my way. And that was the day I knew he was truly my best friend.

Chapter Three

August, 1997

"THIS IS great!" Matt stared out over the lake, where people were out in canoes and kayaks, or roaring past on water skis that followed speedboats. It was a perfect summer morning, and I couldn't agree with him more.

Apparently our misdemeanor was forgiven, although definitely not forgotten. Mom had announced a week ago that it was all arranged for both our families to go camping for a weekend. I think they felt sorry for Matt's family. I was just pleased to spend time with him. His older brother, Darren, had declined to join us—he was at a friend's house for a sleepover. Matt's parents were in one tent with his little sister, and mine were in another. The really great part was that they put me and Matt in a tent together. We'd packed flashlights and snacks and had planned to stay up real late when everyone else had gone to sleep.

Of course, Friday night when we arrived at the campsite, we were so worn out that we fell asleep instantly. So much for that idea.

"Why don't you two boys go for a swim?" his mom suggested. She was sitting on one of the camping chairs my parents had brought, with Matt's sister, Paula, curled up against her.

Okay, yeah, my cheeks grew hot. Matt gave me a sympathetic glance.

"That sounds like a good idea," my dad said with a kind smile, "except that I foresee a slight problem. David hasn't learned to swim yet."

"Really?" Matt's mom stared at me. "I had no idea. Matt swims like a little minnow, has ever since he was four years old."

Matt set his jaw, and I knew what was coming.

"I'm gonna teach David to swim this weekend." His tone was firm.

Yep. Just like I'd thought. Then Mom disappeared into their tent and returned a minute later with a pair of bright orange water wings. I groaned inwardly at the sight of them. I was eight, for heaven's sake!

I did *not* want to be seen wearing objects that I considered were for little kids.

"Aw, that's great." Matt grinned at me. "Just what we need." He took them from her.

I glared at him, wondering if he'd be so pleased if *he* was the one who had to wear them.

Then Matt leaned closer. "Think of it this way. The sooner I get you to swim, the less time you need to wear these."

Now *that* was incentive.

The pair of us went into our tent and changed into our swim trunks. I glanced down at the sky-blue shorts, covered with little sailing boats and gulls, and tried not to groan. "I can't wait till I'm old enough to shop for my own clothes."

Matt cocked his head. "Are those new?" When I nodded, he said, "Think I'd rather have those than have to wear Darren's old ones." His were dark gray, a bit on the long side, and I spied a pin securing them at the waistband.

One look at Matt's glum expression told me it was time to change the subject.

"Okay, time for you to teach me to drown—I mean, swim." I winked at him, and thankfully my words did the trick. He laughed and held up the water wings.

"Arms out."

I did as instructed, waiting patiently while he blew air into them and secured the little rubber stoppers. Then it was time to leave the haven of our tent.

"If anyone giggles…," I muttered as Matt held up the flap of the tent for us to exit.

"No one will do that," Matt assured me. "Your folks are nice people, and that sounds kinda mean."

He was right, of course. No one said a word as I followed Matt to the water's edge.

"Stay where we can see you!" my mom called, her book in her lap. She and Dad were sitting in chairs in front of their tent, with Matt's parents a few feet away in front of theirs.

I nodded and waved at her before kicking off my sandals and stepping carefully into the cool water. I shivered.

Matt must have seen me. "We're gonna walk out a ways, to where it's sunny. The water will be warmer there."

"Not too deep, right?" I gazed out, trying to fathom just how deep it was.

Matt rolled his eyes. "I can't teach you to swim in a couple of inches of water. It needs to be at least up to your waist."

What I liked was the confident way in which he spoke, like it was a foregone conclusion that I'd be swimming before the day was out. Such confidence was contagious.

I squared my shoulders and lifted my chin. "Okay, then. Let's do this." I tried not to look at the orange monstrosities around my biceps. The mud was soft and oozy beneath my feet, squeezing up between my toes. Strange thing was, it didn't feel gross.

When we were several feet from the shore, though still able to see our parents, Matt came to a halt. "This is far enough." The water lapped at our ribs. "I want you to lean forward, as if you're going to lie down on the water. You won't sink, because of the water wings, and I'm gonna put my hands under you to hold you up."

It was my turn to roll my eyes. "I *have* had swimming lessons, y'know."

Matt regarded me steadily, his lips twitching. "Yeah, and they were so successful, right?"

I had no comeback. And before I could think of something, Matt gave me a hard stare.

"Do it. Now."

I obeyed without thinking, surprised by this very different Matt. I kept my chin out of the water, arms outstretched in front of me, and Matt held me up, his arms under my waist.

"Now kick," he said.

I did as I was told, my heart hammering. "You're not gonna let go, are you?" It felt safe, knowing he held me.

"I promise. We're gonna stay like this until we get you used to it." He smiled. "This is better than your swimming lessons, right? We have lots of time. No one is watching. There's no coach breathing down your neck, yelling at you. It's just you and me."

Now I knew why he'd been determined to teach me. This was *so* much better than my swimming lessons, for all the reasons he'd just voiced. "Yeah," I said quietly.

By the time Mom was calling us to get out of the water, my fingers were beginning to prune, but I felt great. I was starting to enjoy the feel of the water, holding me up. I pulled back against the water with cupped hands, and Matt walked slowly with me as I moved. I liked it when Matt got me to close my eyes. I listened to the sounds all around us: the shouts of people farther out on the lake, the dull roar of speedboats, the cries of gulls high in the air above us, and the splash of my feet as they broke the surface of the water.

After a lunch of burgers that Dad cooked on a camping stove, Matt met my gaze. "Ready for more?"

I nodded eagerly, and we dashed out toward the lake. This time I launched myself into the water with no hesitation, Matt's arms around my waist once more.

"I have an idea," Matt said after a few minutes.

I chuckled. "Why am I thinking this is not good?"

"I want to let a little air out of your water wings."

Just like that, my heartbeat sped up. "Really?"

"It'll be fine," he assured me. "You won't even notice, honest."

I wanted to tell him that *hell, yeah*, I'd notice, but there was also the knowledge that I couldn't keep doing this all day. I stood for a moment while Matt fiddled with the stoppers on the water wings.

"I've not let out all that much. See if it feels any different."

I did as before, stretching out on top of the water. To my surprise, he was right. I felt just the same. "You must only have let out a tiny amount." We went back to our earlier activity, me confidently sculling with my hands and kicking my legs, Matt holding me up. A little while later, he repeated the action, and that was the course of our afternoon, right up to the moment when Matt stopped and stared at me.

"You really don't need the water wings anymore," he said earnestly. "There's hardly any air left in them anyway."

"Seriously?" Okay, the idea scared me to death, but there was also an excitement thrumming through me. Was I about to swim, really swim? I stood up in the water, and Matt removed the water wings, folded them, and shoved them into the waistband of his shorts.

"I'll hold you, all right?" he promised. "Until you're ready to try it alone. Only this time, start paddling as soon as you can."

Nodding, I launched myself at the surface of the water and began to paddle, feet kicking strongly. I could feel Matt's arms supporting me.

"Shall I take away one arm?"

There was that excitement again. "Go for it."

I barely felt him remove his arm, I was so intently focused on what my own arms and legs were doing, my head held high. Matt guided me toward the shore, turning my body slowly. "Ready to swim on your own?"

Holy hell. "Yes!" I shouted, my pulse racing. I took a deep breath and paddled for all I was worth, not letting up for a second. Matt was beside me the whole time, yelling encouragements and letting out whoops of delight.

"That's it! You're swimming! You're doing great!"

For a second there, I lost concentration and slipped beneath the surface. I swallowed a mouthful of water in my panic, but then Matt was there, lifting me up, helping me to stand in the knee-high water.

"You did it!"

I felt like I'd conquered Everest. My panic fled, and in its place was pride in my achievement. Matt's arm was around my shoulder as he led me toward the shore, where my parents were standing, both of them applauding. Matt's parents were smiling and clapping too.

It was an amazing feeling, one that I've never forgotten.

"YOU AWAKE?" Matt's whisper crept out of the semidarkness.

I lay in my sleeping bag, watching the moving shapes on the canvas above our heads, made by the firelight beyond. My parents were still up; I could hear the low hum of their voices.

"Yeah," I whispered back. "But we've got to keep quiet. And don't use your flashlight yet. My parents are still outside."

"'Kay. I'm gonna take a peek." There was the rustle as Matt eased out of his sleeping bag, followed by the unmistakable sound of a zipper.

"Don't open the flap too far!" I whispered. Our midnight snacks and stories by flashlight would have to wait until I was sure both my parents were sleeping soundly.

"Damn."

Before I could ask what he meant, their voices drew nearer.

"I'm just going to check on the boys." That was my dad.

"Leave them, honey. If you wake them up, it'll be hours before they get off to sleep again. Besides, there's not been a peep out of them for hours."

I grinned to myself. Matt and I could make like mice when we had to.

"I think Matt was wonderful today." That was my mom. Warmth filled me. I thought he was pretty wonderful too.

"Yeah. Such a pity."

I frowned. What was a pity? That I'd learned to swim? I caught a soft noise from Matt and knew he'd heard too.

"Does he know yet?" My dad again.

"Maryann says they haven't had the heart to tell him. But they'll have to soon. After all, they leave next Saturday."

Matt's soft gasp was clearly audible, and I froze, my heart beating strongly, waiting for them to unzip the flap and find us awake.

"Anyway, it's time we were asleep too."

I waited until I couldn't hear them, then reached under my pillow for my flashlight. When I flicked it on and shone the beam around the tent, it lit up Matt's pale face.

"What did your mom mean about leaving?" His eyes were dark and huge.

"I swear, I have no clue." My belly was in turmoil, and my heart was sinking into it at the prospect of Matt leaving. "Maybe my mom has it all wrong. Maybe she's misunderstood."

The expression on Matt's face told me he wasn't buying it. "I'm gonna go ask my parents."

"Matt, it's the middle of the night," I argued. "This can wait until morning, right? I mean, nothing's gonna happen tonight, is it?"

Matt bit his lip. "I s'pose."

"Look, let's get some sleep. In the morning you can talk to your folks, find out what's going on. Maybe we're worrying about nothing."

Matt blinked. "*We're* worrying about nothing? What have you got to worry about? It's not *your* parents who are probably leaving. You'll still be here, and I'll be God knows where."

I wanted to yell at him. I wanted to say that of *course* I was worried too. I didn't want him to go anywhere. Instead I settled for practicalities. "Right now you don't know that for sure. Well, do you?"

He shook his head, his shoulders hunched over.

"Okay, then go to sleep. And try not to think about it. That won't solve anything." I switched off my flashlight, plunging us into darkness. Outside there was the soft hoot of an owl, probably sitting in the branch of a tree, on the lookout for a hot mouse for his dinner.

Across from me came noises as Matt settled back into his sleeping bag. "Try not to think about it, he says." The quiet murmurings were barely audible.

I knew what he meant, just like I knew I was going to lie awake most of the night, the worry gnawing away at my insides.

THE CLOCK beside my bed glowed in the dark, its red numerals plainly visible. Half past midnight and sleep just wouldn't come. All I could think about was Matt.

He'd said barely a word all day, and I knew my parents had noticed. They'd done their best to involve him in conversations, but with little success. Lunch had been a waste of time, neither of us with a decent appetite between us. I knew he hadn't asked his parents what was going on, and I got that. If it had been me, I'd have been too damned scared to ask, in case it turned out my mom was right all along.

By the time we packed up the tents and all the accompanying stuff that went with camping, he still hadn't brought up the subject, and I guessed he was going to wait until they got home. All evening I stared at the phone, expecting to hear its ring, expecting to be told that Matt was calling to talk to me.

Nothing.

He'll tell me tomorrow at some point, I reasoned. That didn't stop my stomach from clenching, just thinking about what was going on with my friend.

Tap tap tap.

I sat upright in bed, my head jerking toward the window.

There it was again. *Tap tap tap.*

I reached over, switched on the lamp beside me, and got out of bed, my heartbeat pounding as I crossed the floor to pull back the drapes.

Matt stood outside, a bag slung over one shoulder.

I opened the window as quietly and as widely as I could. "What are you doing here?" I whispered.

He stared at me with huge eyes, his chest rising and falling. "Can I climb in?"

What the hell? I nodded and helped him clamber over the windowsill and into my bedroom. He lowered his bag to the floor and regarded me, swallowing.

Jeez, he looked awful.

"What's wrong?" I kept my voice as low as possible. I had no idea how long it had been since my parents went to bed.

"I've run away." Matt gulped and dragged his fingers through his short hair.

"What?" I sat on my bed and he joined me, visibly shaking. "Why?"

"Because I don't want to go to Atlanta," he announced. "I want to stay here, with you."

Oh God. Then it was true. "What did your parents say?"

"Daddy said…." Matt took a moment to breathe. "He said he had a new job, in a factory in Atlanta. Said it was more money than he makes here. Said they'd find me another tutor. Said the schools were better." He swallowed. "They said we're leaving next… Saturday."

"You're going just 'cause your dad found a better job?"

Matt nodded. "He told me and Darren that although they liked it here, things have been pretty tight for a while. They'd been waiting to see if it got better, but then he heard about this other job. Said he couldn't afford to turn it down. So that's it. They're leaving." He squared his jaw in that way of his. "Well, they can leave if they want to. Doesn't mean *I* have to."

My heart went out to him. I wanted him to stay, of course, but I could see problems with his plan. "Your parents won't leave you behind. Where would you live, for one thing?"

"Here." Matt's eyes flashed. "I could live here with you and your folks. There's plenty of room." His gaze flickered around the room. "We could even share."

"Don't you think your parents would miss you?"

Matt snorted. "Why would they? It's not like they even know I'm gone, now is it?"

When I caught the sound of the phone ringing in my parents' room and the low rumble of my dad's voice, I knew instinctively who was calling. "I wouldn't be so sure about that."

Matt opened his eyes wide. "Quick. Where can I hide?"

I pointed to the closet, knowing deep down it was going to be futile. Matt lurched up off the bed, dashed across the room, and closed the door behind him. Seconds later there was a tap on my door and my mom poked her head around it. She glanced at my room and then came in.

"Sweetheart, is Matt here?"

I blinked. "Matt? No, of course not. Why would Matt be here?"

Mom pointed to Matt's school bag, standing in the middle of the floor. "Because that is not yours, and you're sitting here with the light on." Before I could say a word, she walked across to my closet and pulled open the door.

Her face fell. "Come on out, honey."

What surprised me was that she didn't appear angry.

Matt came out unhurriedly, and she knelt down in front of him. "Matt, honey, your mom just called. They were frightened when they looked in on you and found you weren't there. When they saw you'd taken some clothes and your bag, this was the first place they thought of. They're on their way now to pick you up."

Matt's lower lip trembled. "But... I don't want to go." He swallowed hard.

Mom stroked his cheek. "I know, baby, I know. But you have to. You'll see. Things will turn out all right when you get to Atlanta. And anytime you want to talk to David, you just tell your mom and dad, and they'll let you, okay?"

Dad appeared in the doorway. "Maryann is here." He gave me a look that seemed sad, like he knew how I was feeling. "Say good night to David. You'll see him tomorrow, all right?"

Matt nodded, his eyes dull. My mom stood up and stepped to one side as Matt went toward the door. "See you tomorrow," he said to me, not meeting my gaze, before disappearing from my sight. Dad followed him.

I blinked. "He's really leaving?"

Mom sat on my bed, her hand curled around mine. "Yes, sweetheart. I know this feels awful right now, but it will get better."

A brief flare of frustration passed through me. "Yeah? And how do you know that? Did you have *your* best friend move away?" I couldn't believe I'd had the nerve to say that to her, but damn it, I was hurting too.

"David, you'll make other friends. I promise."

"You don't know that," I insisted, with all the superior knowledge of an eight-year-old boy. "And I don't want other friends. I want Matt."

She stroked my hair gently. "Turn out the light and go to sleep. You can get up early and go see him. You have to make the most of this week, before he leaves." She got up from the bed and went toward the door. "Good night, David."

I lay down after turning the light off, and stared at the ceiling.

Like I needed reminding that he was going.

"MATT'S HERE."

I put down my book and got up from the table. All morning I'd wanted to go to his house, to help them pack up all their belongings into the van his dad had hired, but Dad had told me to stay away.

Matt stepped into the kitchen. "Hey. I came to say goodbye."

Dad held out his hand, and Matt shook it. "It's been good to have you around, son. Stay in touch, you hear?"

Matt nodded and then turned to my mom. "Thank you, Mrs. Lennon. You've been really nice."

She ruffled Matt's hair and kissed his forehead. "It's been a pleasure having you around. Good luck in Atlanta." Her gaze flicked toward me. "Maybe David can walk you home—back to the house, I mean."

K.C. Wells

My gut clenched. Yeah. It wasn't Matt's home anymore.

I nodded, forcing a smile. "That sounds good." I followed Matt to the door and told my parents I'd be back soon. Then we stepped out into the bright August sunlight.

"Have your parents found a house?" I asked as we walked along.

"They've found a place to rent. Dad says it's better, seeing as they haven't sold the house yet."

I could see the For Sale sign at the end of their driveway, along with the large white van and their car. "Everything packed?" I knew I was just making small talk, but I didn't have a clue what to say. The thought of Matt getting into one of the two vehicles and pulling away from 465 South Segoe Road filled me with a quiet ache.

"Yeah. I'm still amazed they got it all in."

His brother, Darren, was standing at the roadside, talking earnestly with a girl. "Bet Darren's not happy about leaving."

Matt huffed. "He's whined about it all week."

"And you haven't?"

Matt turned his head in my direction. "Me? I've been quiet. Half the time it didn't feel real."

I could understand that.

We reached the house and his mom came out, his sister, Paula, in her arms. "Hey, David. Nice of you to come see us off. We're just about ready to leave." She walked over to the car, placed Paula in the back, and fastened her into the child seat.

Matt's dad glanced over at Darren. "Time to go, son."

Darren pulled a face, then leaned over to kiss the girl on the cheek. With a sullen glance at his dad, he climbed into the cab of the van and slammed the door shut.

Matt's dad sighed. "Great. It's sure gonna be fun riding all the way to Atlanta with him in this mood."

I said nothing. I didn't trust myself.

He nodded toward me. "Thanks for coming, David. Good luck in the future. You're a smart kid—you'll go far." With that, he got into the van too.

Matt's mom came over to me, her hand held out. When I took it, she clasped it between hers. "I need to thank you before we go."

"For what?" I genuinely had no clue.

She smiled. "It was you who put the idea in Matt's head to get him tested about his reading, wasn't it?"

Oh. That. "It was just an idea."

"Yes, but it changed everything. Thank you for that." She released my hand and gestured toward the car. "Time to go, Matt."

Matt faced me, blinking rapidly. "Goodbye, David. I hope we stay in touch."

"Me too."

The pair of us regarded each other, an awkwardness descending. Then he got into the front seat next to his mom. I watched them pull away from the curb and head down the street, Matt's hand sticking out of the window as he waved.

I waited until they were no longer in sight, and then I turned to head home.

NOTE

GOD, I wanted to hug him. I wanted to wrap my arms around him and hold him tight, but I couldn't. What was more, I got the feeling he wanted to do the same. I'm not sure what gave it away. Maybe it was the look of longing on his face, the way he raised his arms ever so slightly.

I wished he had, but that day, neither of us was brave enough.

Chapter Four

DESPITE OUR best intentions, communication between us sort of dried up.

We started out okay. For the first month, we spoke on the phone every Saturday. Then it got to be every couple of weeks. Then once a month. I'd talk about what I was doing in school, and Matt would tell me what was happening in his life. Apparently, everything wasn't going to plan. For one thing, the tutor his parents had promised never materialized. It sounded as though he wasn't doing so well in school. And it definitely sounded like none of them were particularly happy in Atlanta. I wanted to yell into the phone, *Then come back!* Except, of course, I knew it wasn't that easy.

It got so that I became accustomed to the sporadic phone calls. At least I still heard from him. There was no one to step into his sneakers and fill the void he'd left behind, however. I entered fourth grade determined to do well, and concentrated on being the best at everything. I took up new hobbies, tried to develop new interests, and managed to do well in my studies. There was one area where I sucked—making friends.

To be honest, I can't remember much about fourth grade. It's kind of a blur. You ever have years like that? Where nothing stands out, no earth-shattering events, where life blends into a sort of *meh* existence?

No, what sticks out in my memory is that day at the beginning of fifth grade, maybe in October, when Mrs. Portman came into the classroom one morning and announced that we were getting a new student. Then she clarified her statement to say that it wasn't so much a *new* student as a returning one.

I almost fell over when Matt walked through the door.

I gaped as he strolled toward the back of the room where there was an empty desk and plonked himself down into the chair. Our gazes met across the classroom and he grinned, mouthing, *Surprise.*

Surprise? I was *so* gonna give him a surprise when recess arrived.

Of course, that morning dragged, despite my best efforts to wish away the hours. Finally the bell rang, and I leaped to my feet.

Mrs. Portman, unfortunately, had other ideas. "David? Can you stay behind, please?"

Damn. I sighed inwardly, watching Matt leave the room, and trudged reluctantly to her desk. As it turned out, all she wanted was to ask if I'd consider writing an article for the student newspaper. I was honored to be asked and said as much. I couldn't recall reading *anything* written by an elementary school student. She told me she'd leave the topic to me and then let me go.

I ran out of the door and into the yard, scanning the area for Matt among the maze of kids playing there. Then it occurred to me that I knew exactly where to look.

I bolted across the field toward the old tree. Sure enough, Matt was standing beneath it, smiling, like he knew I'd turn up.

"Sorry I didn't call to—"

That was as far as he got before I launched myself at him and grabbed him in a fierce hug. "You got taller," I whispered, unwilling to let go in case he up and disappeared on me.

Matt chuckled. "Yeah. So did you."

I released him, then delivered a swift punch to his arm.

"Ow! What's that for?" He glared at me, rubbing his arm.

"*That* is for not telling me you were moving back." I returned his glare. "When did you know you were coming?"

"Daddy didn't tell us until three nights ago. I meant to call, but Momma said it could wait—there was too much to do. She said you'd know I was back when I got here." He grinned. "I guess she was right."

We sat on the grass. I couldn't believe I'd hugged him, but then, I reasoned, he'd hugged me too. "So. What happened?"

Matt sighed. "The factory closed, Daddy lost his job, and he had real problems trying to find a new one. Turns out my folks had been talking about moving back for a while. They just didn't tell us anything. The school was nothing like Van Hise, and they didn't think I was doing as well. I didn't have a tutor, and apparently the waiting list was huge." He shrugged. "I guess it all added up to one big 'Hey, we made a mistake.'

We're renting a house a few blocks from here, so I'm a little farther away than before. Daddy says we're not buying a house until things get more settled."

Like I cared. I had my best friend back in my life.

"This is for good, right? I mean, they're not gonna tell you in a few months or a year's time that you're leaving again?" There was only so much a boy could take, you know what I mean?

Matt shrugged. "Who knows? Right now I'm just happy we're back. I can't wait to hear what you got up to while I was gone." His eyes twinkled. "Like, have you pushed anyone into a bathroom sink lately?"

I groaned, but before I could remind him that no pushing had been involved, the bell rang for the end of recess. "Come over to my house tonight after school?" I asked as we ran across the field toward the school building.

"Sure. I'll go home and tell Momma first. I can't see her minding much."

I could see *my* mom being delighted. That was, unless she already knew. I recalled her manner that morning as she'd sent me off to school. She'd been suspiciously cheerful, and I'd briefly wondered what was going on.

Seemed like I had my answer.

"SO, TELL me about Atlanta. What was it like?" The pair of us were sprawled on my bed as aromas from the kitchen seeped under my door. Matt had gotten permission to stay for dinner.

He shook his head. "Way too big for me. The city was enormous. I hated it when we went shopping, not that we went all that often."

I guessed money was still tight.

"What about your school? Did you make many friends?"

Another shrug. "There *was* one girl I spent a lot of time with, and—"

I stared at him. "You got yourself a girlfriend? Don't you think ten is too young for that?" I knew it was bogus as soon as I said it. Clara Dean and Luke Monroe were sweet on each other, and they were in the fifth grade too. But something tightened in my belly at the thought of Matt finding himself a new best friend.

Matt winced. "Ellie wasn't my girlfriend. *Jeez*. She was a friend who happened to be a girl. And I was sure glad to have her around, because most of the kids in that school were either stuck-up or just plain weird. Don't know what I'd have done if she hadn't been there. I'd have been a damn sight lonelier, that's for sure."

A pang of guilt pierced me. "Sorry I didn't call that much."

Matt waved his hand. "You were here, I was there—what else is there to say? I figured you had stuff going on, same as me. And it wasn't just you, was it? I could've called more often, right?" He smiled. "Doesn't matter now, 'cause I'm back." He gave me an almost shy look. "What about you? Did you get yourself a new best friend?" He didn't break eye contact, like he was dying to know what was going to come out of my mouth.

I snickered. "You've seen who's in that class. Most of the kids have been there since we met in second grade. You seriously telling me there's one kid among them who could hold a candle to you?" I grinned. "The job's yours, if you want it."

Matt heaved a sigh of relief. "I'll take it."

There was a tap on the door, and Mom poked her head around it, smiling. "Are there any boys in here who like fried chicken with mashed potatoes and gravy?" Then she ducked out of the way to prevent herself from being mowed down by two ravenous kids.

Matt got grilled over dinner, of course. It was fun watching him trying to answer my parents' questions while stuffing chicken into his mouth like chickens were about to go extinct. Especially as he was a polite kid who never spoke with his mouth full.

"Did David tell you he's taken up fishing?" my dad asked toward the end of the meal.

Matt stared at me across the table and blinked. "Fishing? That sounds… great."

I knew what he meant to say. I could read it in his eyes.

"Yes, I took him to the lake in late spring and taught him how to fish." Dad smiled. "Maybe you might like to join him."

Okay, now I was interested. "Really?" I sat up, my back ramrod straight.

"I was thinking about driving you two to the lake this Saturday, once you've finished your chores. I could lend Matt a rod, and you could show him the ropes. I figure I can trust you to be on your own for a few hours. Of course, you'd have to ask your parents for permission."

Mom nodded enthusiastically. "I think that's a great idea. I could pack you a cooler with some sandwiches and bottles of pop."

This was sounding better and better. I gazed across at Matt, who was almost bouncing on his seat. Yeah, he liked the idea too.

"Can I call my mom and ask her now?"

Scrap that. He loved it.

WE SAT on little camping stools, both of us bundled up in thick jackets. It seemed both our moms had insisted, once the day had turned out a little chilly. The fishing rods were stuck into the soft earth, their lines trailing out into the lake, but so far, not so much as a nibble.

We didn't care. We were on our own, no parents for at least a couple of hours, and outside in the bright October sunshine. The leaves still on the trees glowed in the light, gorgeous oranges and reds, and there was a thick carpet of them beneath our feet. A little blue cooler sat between us, and we'd already drunk a bottle of pop each. Mom's meatloaf sandwiches were still to come.

Life didn't get any more perfect than that.

Matt peered out at the lake. "Have you ever caught anything?"

I nodded. "Nothing too big, and to be honest, if they were tiny, I threw them back in." It had felt cruel once I'd seen them dancing on the end of my line. I reached into the cooler. "More pop?"

"Sure." Matt glanced around. "Only, there are no restrooms near here." The area where we sat was devoid of people, although there were a few boats out on the lake, zipping through the waves and skidding into wide turns, leaving trails in the water.

I giggled. "That's what bushes are for." I pointed to the water. "And there's always the lake."

Matt's eyes widened. "I am *not* peeing in the lake. I *swim* in there."

I burst into laughter, and Matt huffed.

After we'd spent another half an hour with nothing to show for it—according to the brand-new Timex I'd gotten for my birthday—I figured it was time to eat. We ate our sandwiches, and I discovered a couple of packets of chips that Mom had hidden under them. We sure weren't going to starve.

"Is Darren happy to be back?"

Matt laughed. "He isn't. He was whining about us leaving Atlanta, but I'm not sure why. He's going to college there, and he's staying in the dorms. Can you see Darren missing me?"

I snorted. "Not really."

"Mind you...." Matt sat up and glanced around us, his manner almost furtive.

"What? What are you up to?"

Matt unzipped his jacket and reached inside it. "I've brought something," he whispered.

I snickered. "Why are you whispering?" But I saw exactly why when he placed a rolled-up, battered-looking magazine on my lap, which unfurled itself to reveal....

"*Playboy*?" Now I was the one whispering. On the cover was a woman dressed in black panties and stockings, with a see-through top that meant you could see *everything*. I gaped. "Where did you get this?"

"It's one of Darren's," Matt informed me. "And you should see inside it."

Gingerly, as if touching the cover would result in an electric shock, I lifted it and—

Oh my God.

It was *full* of women.

Women wearing sexy underwear. Women wearing nothing at all, except for a pair of high-heeled shoes. Tits of all sizes, some of them impossibly large. But most shocking were the images of women with their legs spread, revealing everything that lay between them.

Matt shifted closer and peered over my shoulder. "Did you think they'd look like that?" he whispered.

I stared at the shocking photos. Women on their hands and knees, peering over their shoulders, their asses pointed toward the camera.

Women touching themselves… *there*. "I wasn't sure," I admitted. I couldn't tear my eyes away. It felt really wicked, sinful, and… riveting.

"Darren had lots of these. I snuck this one out of his room when we were packing and hid it in my stuff." Matt shuddered. "There was this one moment when I felt sure Momma was gonna find it. I thought I was gonna have a heart attack."

I could understand that.

"I heard Darren talking with his friends sometimes," Matt confided. "Especially when two or three of them came to the house and they'd go into the yard to smoke a cigarette." He chuckled. "Darren is such an idiot. Who smokes by an open window?"

Yeah, I could believe that about Darren.

"They used to talk a lot," Matt continued. "Saying how cool it was."

"How cool what was?"

Matt rolled his eyes. "Darren's done it. *You* know… it."

For a moment I was perplexed, and then the light dawned. "Ohhhh." I stared at the images. "Eww. With that? I don't get it."

"Me neither," Matt confessed. "But don't they look…?" He shivered. "Not really sure *how* they look."

And I was suddenly sure that I didn't want to look anymore. I hastily rolled up the magazine and thrust it into his hand. "Put it away." I took a look around, making sure there was no one in sight.

Matt tucked it back inside his jacket, and then his eyes widened. "You've got a bite!"

I jerked my head to look at my rod, and sure enough, the line bobbed as something below the surface tugged at it. "Yay!" I got to my feet, grabbed the rod, and reeled in the line as fast as I could. A large silvery fish burst through the water, rainbows shimmering over it as the sunlight danced over its scales. "Look at that!"

Matt laughed. "You're not throwing *that* one back!"

"Are you kidding me? Wait till my dad sees this!" I reeled in more line, and Matt hastened to grab the net, then held it out below the wriggling fish. When he had it safely contained, Matt placed the net on the ground, staring at it.

"It's still moving," he said quietly.

This was the part I usually hated when Dad and I went fishing, but I knew it had to be done. "Not for long." I grasped the net, feeling the fish's slippery skin beneath it, and aimed its head toward the nearest rock. One well-aimed slap and the fish lay still.

Matt's eyes were large and round. "You killed it."

I groaned inwardly. "I couldn't leave it. That would've been cruel. It was suffocating out of the water. At least I put it out of its misery."

Matt didn't look convinced. "I s'pose."

I sighed as I laid the fish on the ground. "It's okay. I know how you feel. I felt the same way the first time I watched my dad do it. How do you think I felt when he made *me* do it? But he was right. There are some things you just have to get used to, even though you might not like doing them."

Matt fell silent for a moment. "Fair enough." He peered at the fish and shuddered. "Although it's enough to make you consider becoming a vegetarian."

I had to laugh at that. "Can't see *you* doing that anytime soon. I've seen the way you eat chicken."

It wasn't long before Matt was laughing too.

NOTE

I SUPPOSE every man remembers his introduction to sex. That first glimpse of something illicit, the way it makes your heartbeat race and your blood rush. Both Matt and I had glimpsed nude women, of course. A flash now and again on the TV screen, accompanied by a quick peek to see if our parents had noticed, because we didn't want to be caught looking. But that was our first full-on experience of porn, albeit soft porn, with nothing left to the imagination.

Years later we'd laugh at that notion that what we'd seen was truly all there was.

Yeah, we were only ten, after all.

Chapter Five

Early June, 2002

WHEN MATT had first brought up the idea of mowing lawns to earn money, I was all for it. I got an allowance, but only if I did my chores around the house. I had to keep my bedroom tidy, make sure I cleaned up after myself in my bathroom, empty the dishwasher and put everything away, and take out the trash. Of course, I knew deep down that if I failed to do any of my allotted tasks, that wouldn't mean an end to my allowance—Mom would say something, and I'd feel like shit, but that would be the extent of it. Matt's parents, on the other hand, couldn't afford to give him an allowance, so when he came up with the idea, I was right behind him.

Only, I hadn't given it much thought.

I asked my dad if I could use his computer to make flyers to advertise Matt's new venture. I knew Dad wouldn't mind, and sure enough, he nodded enthusiastically. Matt and I spent a few hours one night after school hunting for pictures to accompany the text. When he saw the finished result, Matt was delighted. We spent another evening printing out the flyers, three to a page, and then cutting them up.

The following weekend we each took a bundle of flyers and went around the entire neighborhood, shoving them into mailboxes and sticking them on lampposts and everywhere we found a flat surface. Then we sat back and waited for the calls to come in.

Okay, so it was slow at first. Matt had maybe one or two calls the next week, and we stared glumly at the paltry sum in his money jar. Then word got around. It seemed no one gave a shit about the flyers—word of mouth was a *lot* more powerful.

Then things really took off.

I went from being extremely supportive to extremely pissed off. Matt was never available when I wanted to do something on the weekends—he was too busy mowing other people's lawns. After a few weeks of this, I joked that if I wanted to spend time with him outside of school, I'd have to pay him to mow our lawn. Matt had snickered at that.

Except I wasn't joking.

It went on like this for months. And on those rare occasions when he wasn't mowing a lawn, he was visiting… garage sales.

Garage sales? Really?

I was starting to think my best friend didn't want to spend time with me.

What made it worse was that my manner changed toward Matt. I reasoned that if making money was more important to him than being with me, then so be it. He was welcome to spend his spare time mowing, clipping, whatever the hell he was doing. I'd keep my own company, thank you very much. Let Matt go to every garage sale he could find, because that was sure how it looked to me. Besides, I had enough on my plate, trying to maintain my academic success in eighth grade. Ninth grade was looming ever closer.

Once school was out for the summer, Matt carried on with his rapidly growing business. Does grass grow faster in the summertime? Because he sure was mowing an awful lot of lawns. I'd pictured the two of us camping, fishing, spending time together, but instead I saw less and less of him, and I resented him for it. I'd gone to the movies a couple of times with him, sure, but it wasn't the same anymore.

The truth was, of course, that I missed him.

SUMMER WAS almost over that Saturday when Matt came to the house. Only he didn't come to the front door. Instead, he came tap-tap-tapping on my bedroom window. I peered through it at him, standing there in his jeans and T-shirt, his hands behind his back.

I opened the window and arched my eyebrows. "Let me guess. You're running away and you've come to say goodbye."

Matt's smile was kind of sad. "God, that seems like such a long time ago now."

"What are you doing here? There's still daylight enough to find a lawn to mow," I joked, only it sounded mean to my ears, like I was poking him.

Maybe that was how it sounded to Matt too, because he winced. "Yeah, about that. I'm sorry I've not had a lot of spare time this summer. I was kinda busy."

"I did notice."

Matt's eyes flashed. "Right, but I'm here now." He cocked his head to one side. "Am I still your best friend?"

God, I was *that* close to telling him friends actually spent time together, but I put a brake on my mouth. Besides, there was no one who came close to him.

I snorted. "You make us sound like we're little kids." Hell, we were fourteen, well and truly teenagers. But one look at Matt's earnest expression killed any desire to be a smart-mouth. "Yeah," I admitted quietly. "There haven't been any other applicants for the position, so I guess it's still you." I couldn't resist one little poke.

"Mm-hmm." Matt gave me that smile of his, the one that always made me think he was up to something. "Okay, open your hands and close your eyes and you will get a big surprise."

I laughed. "Maybe one of us is still a kid after all." Nevertheless I did as instructed, recoiling slightly when something hard and cool was placed into my hands. Two somethings, actually. Then the somethings moved, and I jerked my eyes open.

In my upturned palms sat two little turtles.

I stared at them, watching as, one at a time, they poked out their little leathery heads and stretched their necks. "Oh wow." My throat tightened.

"Well, you always wanted one, but I figured two was better. Company for each other."

I blinked. "You got these… for me."

Matt chuckled. "That *was* you who made us go hunting for turtles, right?"

I didn't know what else to say. I was so touched by the thoughtfulness of Matt's gift. Then the practical part of my brain kicked in. "What am I supposed to do with them like this? Let them sleep in my bed?" I was joking, of course, but inside I was racking my brains for where to put my new little friends.

"How about you put them in this?" Matt stepped to one side, and I saw what sat on the lawn behind him. It was a large glass tank.

"You got me an aquarium too? Jeez, Matt, this must have cost you a fortune."

Matt's face flushed. "Sorry, but it's not a new one. I found it at a garage sale."

Now it all made sense. "That's why you went to all those sales? Looking for an aquarium?"

He nodded. "I had to make sure I had one before I bought the turtles." Matt grinned. "And no, they're not secondhand."

"You didn't spend all the money you made mowing lawns on these, did you?" I was beginning to feel bad.

His face flushed a deeper shade of red. "Not all, no. Besides, most of the money I earn, I give it to Momma. My way of helping out."

Yeah, you can guess how that made me feel, right? Very, very small.

His gaze met mine. "You do like them?"

I had to reassure him on that. "Matt, it's wonderful. Thank you so much."

Matt let out a happy little sigh. "Okay, then put the turtles on your bed and help me get the aquarium through the window."

I raised my eyebrows. "How about we bring it through the front door, y'know, like normal people?"

Matt shrugged. "That works too." He grinned. "I'll meet you there."

I deposited my little guys on the bed, then returned to the window to close it, shaking my head. Matt was truly amazing, and I was such a lucky guy.

NOTE

READING BACK over that last part, a couple of things occurred to me, the most important one being the revelation that I was a selfish prick. No other description will suffice.

What else occurred to me?

Matt is probably the most unselfish person I've ever known. He took on that job not only to raise enough money to buy me a couple of turtles, but also to give money to his parents, because he knew times were hard. And knowing Matt, I'll bet you anything you like that he gave away most of it.

What he didn't know at the time—we only found out years later—was that his mom didn't spend a dime of that money. Instead, she saved every nickel in a fund, a sort of Matt Emergency Fund, for when he'd need money in the future.

Aren't some parents amazing? They let him work, helping him develop independence. They made him feel valuable by allowing him to help them out, when of course they had no intention of touching any of it. And when the time came, they gave it back to him, providing him with yet more independence when he truly needed it.

Such a simple act as mowing lawns, and yet it had so many layers.

Chapter Six

Fall, 2004

ONE SEMESTER into eleventh grade, both our lives changed significantly, and Matt's brother, Darren, proved to be the unknowing catalyst.

It began innocently enough, with Darren teasing him about his lack of a girlfriend. Darren was then at the lofty age of twenty-three, a seasoned veteran when it came to affairs of the heart.

I told Matt to pay him no mind. "No one cares if you don't have a girlfriend," I assured him. "And besides, why would you want to listen to Darren? He goes through girls like most of us go through a tube of toothpaste."

Matt snickered at that. "It seems like every time he comes home, he has a different girl with him. Mom says she's losing count, and Dad says he's waiting for the day when Darren tells them he's gonna be a dad himself."

That wouldn't surprise me.

It was during Darren's next visit that things changed, however.

Matt and I were in my bedroom, both of us with our heads stuck in a book, preparing for a test. I lay on the bed, pillows stuffed behind my head, and Matt was on the rug, looking like the beanbag he was sitting in was trying to swallow him. Mom had brought us pop and snacks and then left us to it.

Matt's words came out of the blue, breaking the comfortable silence. "Darren asked me if I was gay last night."

I jerked my head up. "He asked what? Seriously?" I stared at Matt, whose cheeks were flushed. "Why the fuck would he ask that?"

Matt arched his eyebrows. "Better not let your mom hear you say that. Remember what happened last time?"

Oh yeah. Mom had slapped me upside the head when I said "shit."

I lowered my voice. "Don't change the subject. Did he really ask you that?"

Matt nodded. "And it's not the first time."

I sighed heavily. "God, he talks a lot of shit sometimes. Is this the whole you-don't-have-a-girlfriend thing again?"

"Yep."

I growled at him. "You don't *need* a girlfriend."

There was an awkward silence. "Maybe he's just worried about me."

I huffed impatiently. "Asking you if you're gay sounds like a weird way of worrying about you, if you ask me."

Matt put down his book and sat up, facing me. "Have you heard what's going on with Thomas Mitchell?"

Oh hell. Suddenly I knew where he was going with this.

There were rumors flying all around the school that Thomas was gay. No one was sure how they got started, but we couldn't help but notice how they'd taken off. Thomas had denied it, at times vehemently, but that didn't stop the rumor mill from grinding out tale after tale, until he couldn't walk down the hall without someone calling out after him.

Faggot.

Queer.

Gay.

And worse.

God, high school kids could be cruel.

"Thomas is not the only one, of course," Matt said quietly. "If some of them so much as suspect a student of being gay, they give the poor guy hell. It doesn't matter whether he is or isn't, the result is the same."

I knew he spoke the truth. I hated it, but that accomplished nothing.

Matt sighed, picked up his book, and gave a nod toward mine. "Let's get back to preparing for Monday's test, Mr. Top of the Class." He gave me a half smile. "You have a rep to maintain, after all."

I smiled, but something deep in my belly rolled over, and I couldn't get over the feeling that something important had just happened.

January, 2005.

"So, what do you want to do this Saturday? The movies? Bowling?" I asked. Lunchtime was nearly over, and it wouldn't be long until Friday was at an end and the weekend was upon us.

Matt cleared his throat. "Actually, I have a date."

I paused, my bottle of water halfway to my mouth. "Date?" I blinked. "Who with?"

A moment's silence. "Cathy Jordan."

I stared. Blinked again. "Cathy Jordan? Really?" Cathy was quite possibly the mousiest girl in our year. She was intelligent, sure, but a plainer girl I hadn't laid eyes on.

Matt stared at me. "And what does that tone mean?"

"What tone?" I feigned innocence.

When Matt arched one eyebrow, I knew I was in trouble. "You know perfectly well what tone I mean. Cathy's nice."

"I'm sure she is. I just had no idea you knew each other. You've certainly never mentioned her."

Matt smirked. "I don't have to tell you everything, do I?"

"No," I said slowly. "It's just…." I wasn't sure how best to frame my thoughts.

"What?" Matt folded his arms across his chest. "Come on. Spit it out."

"She just seems an… odd choice."

Matt's lips twitched. "Oh? And who do *you* think I should be asking on a date? Donna Anderson?"

God, I nearly spluttered my water all over my lunch. Donna was only the most popular girl in the school, but you tangled with her at your peril. She chewed boys up and spat them out.

"She wouldn't be my first choice," I said, wiping my mouth with a napkin. "So, tell me about Cathy. When did you ask her out?" This was still a shock. I supposed I shouldn't have been surprised that Matt was dating someone. He was a good-looking guy, with a good sense of humor and a keen mind.

"We were in the library. We both went to take out the same book, so I suggested a compromise. We're going to study it together after school." He shrugged. "Then I asked if she'd like to go to the movies. She said yes."

"I see." There was something niggling away at me, something I couldn't put my finger on.

"So, yeah. Sorry about that. Maybe we can go see a movie next weekend?" Matt suggested.

"Yeah, sure." I gave him a bright smile that was pure show. I told myself I was being selfish. I told myself that it was only one Saturday, for God's sake.

Except it wasn't.

May, 2005

"WHAT DO you have planned for this weekend?" Mom asked me over dinner.

I helped myself to more potatoes. "I have a long list. I have to read the minutes of the last meeting of the student council before Wednesday's meeting. Then I need to make notes for Friday's debate. I've got the layout of the school newspaper to look over for the end of the month. And we still have to finalize details for the yearbook. I mean, it's coming out in a couple of weeks." I was a busy, busy boy.

Mom glanced across at my dad, and something passed between them. The skin on my arms prickled. "What's wrong?"

Mom put down her fork. "We're a little concerned, that's all."

"About what?"

Dad regarded me in silence for a moment, until all the hairs on my arms stood on end. Was I missing something?

"You seem to have a lot on your plate, that's all," he said gently. "President of the student council. You run the school newspaper. You're on the yearbook committee. The debate team. You're a member of the photography club. Not to mention all the studying you do." He tilted his head to one side. "We're not telling you to quit any of those activities, because they're all good things, stuff that will look great on a resume, but…."

"But?"

Mom cleared her throat. "We're just worried that you might have taken on too much." Her gaze met mine. "How's Matt?"

The question was so out of the blue that it caught me off guard. "Matt?"

She smiled. "You know. Matt, your best friend since you were eight? The other half of David-and-Matt, the Dynamic Duo?" Her smile faltered. "We haven't seen much of him lately. We wondered if anything had happened between you."

"Nothing's happened," I assured her. "He just spends a lot of time with Cathy these days." My chest tightened.

"Sounds like it's kind of serious between those two." Dad's gaze was focused on me.

I couldn't say a word, because that was exactly how it looked to me too.

"You miss him, don't you?" Mom's voice was kind.

God, that was such an understatement.

I swallowed. "It was all round school last week that Cathy was wearing a ring with Matt's initials engraved on it." What I didn't tell them was that the same rumor also had it that he was wearing a ring with her initials on it.

"Oh. Oh, I see." Mom's eyes held so much compassion that my heart ached to see it. "That does sound serious. You never know where those high school romances will lead." She regarded my dad lovingly, who chuckled and gave her hand a squeeze.

With a shock I realized why she was looking at him like that. They'd been high school sweethearts. They'd gotten engaged at the end of twelfth grade and married about six months after that.

Matt—and Cathy?

NOTE

I KNEW why I threw myself into every available club, of course. I'd picked the perfect distraction technique for me. Everyone knew I was an overachiever. No one questioned why I was doing so much. So no one asked even once why *I* didn't have a girlfriend. They just assumed I was too busy to have a relationship.

No one knew that I was keeping myself busy to fill the void left by Matt. It wasn't until that year that I realized just how much time we'd spent together, and I was feeling the loss.

I'm ashamed to admit, when Matt first told me he'd asked Cathy on a date, my first thought had been that she was merely a decoy, a prop so that he could avoid all the shit Thomas had gone through. But as the months went by and they grew closer, I had to reassess the situation. Maybe I had him all wrong. Maybe he genuinely cared for her.

And if that was true, then the chasm between us had just widened.

Chapter Seven

July, 2005

"WHAT ARE you doing?" Mom asked me as she came into the living room.

I was sitting on the couch, scanning the newspapers laid out over the coffee table. "Looking for a job." I was a week into the summer vacation, and I needed the distraction a job would provide. I'd sort of resigned myself to not having Matt around much. Sort of. It was like I was missing an arm, or something. I was left with a vague ache in my heart and an awful big hole in my life.

Mom sat down next to me. "I don't think you should work this summer."

I turned my head to regard her with wide eyes. "Seriously? I'd have thought you'd be glad to have me out from under your feet." I grinned.

Mom reached over to ruffle my hair, but I ducked out of the way, and she laughed. "Your dad and I have been talking. You have some big decisions to make this coming year, like which college to go to, for one. You should relax this summer. It might be your last chance to do that for a while. I assume you'll get a job while you're in college and for the breaks, so yes, call this your last summer before real life kicks your butt." She smiled. "What do you think?"

I liked the idea, sure, but....

"Don't get me wrong, I think it's cool, but I'm not sure what I'd do with myself for the whole summer." I kept in the words that should have followed: *now that Matt isn't around so much.*

"I've been thinking about that too." Mom tilted her head, her gaze speculative. "I think you need a camping trip."

I was about to tell her that, nice though the idea of spending time with her and Dad was, I wasn't a kid anymore. Then her words registered. "Wait a minute. *I* need a camping trip?" I smiled. "Sounds a little lonely, Mom."

She smiled, her eyes sparkling. "Oh, I didn't mean for you to go on your own. I think you and Matt should go."

I stilled. "I don't think he'd go for it, to be honest."

Mom got up from the couch. "Well, you'll never know if you don't ask him. Why don't you call him and find out?" And with that she left me and went into the kitchen. "Lunch in ten minutes," she called out.

I sagged against the seat cushions. Matt would never go for it. Oh, once upon a time, maybe, before he got himself loved up, but not now.

Yeah. I missed him.

The phone rang. "I'll get it," I yelled to Mom. Dad was in the workshop at the back of the garage, trying to fix one of the kitchen chairs. "Hey, this is David."

"Hey. How are you?"

"Matt?" We hadn't spoken since school had finished for the summer the previous week. "Hey, buddy." For once I was at a loss for words.

"You got any plans for the summer?"

I had to smile. "Funny you should ask. Mom and I were just talking about that very subject."

"Yeah? Me too. Actually, Momma had a great idea."

You know how sometimes you get like a sixth sense about stuff? Like you know what's going to happen before it does?

"Let me guess. You and me, going on a camping trip."

Silence at the other end of the line. "How did you know?" Matt half whispered. "Who are you, Richard Osterlind's missing brother?"

I laughed. "Who?"

"Some mentalist I was reading about, but never mind that. How did you know?"

"For someone who's as smart as you are, you can be pretty slow on the uptake. Our moms have been talking, dude."

Matt chuckled. "Duh. Of course. That makes sense." He paused. "Well, what do you think of the idea?"

The fact that he was calling me about it sent a hopeful flutter through my insides. "I like it. We could fish, swim, read, do whatever we wanted." I waited, my heartbeat racing just a little. *Come on, Matt, say yes.* I didn't want to pressure him, but yeah, the more I thought about it, the more I loved the idea.

"I thought it sounded like a neat idea too. So I guess we pick a week?"

Wait—what? "Really?"

"Sure."

"But…." I was dying to ask. *But what about your girlfriend? Won't she mind?* Then I figured if he wasn't going to bring her up, then neither was I. "Fine. Let's choose a week." The kitchen door opened and Mom came through with our lunch. "Hey, sorry, but I'm gonna have to cut this short. Lunchtime."

"Sure thing. I'll call you later and we can talk dates."

"Great." I said goodbye and hung up.

"Was that Matt?"

I took one look at Mom's innocent expression and laughed. "Like you didn't know."

She smiled. "Aw, I'm glad he liked the idea too. It's about time the two of you reconnected."

I followed her to the table. "What do you mean?"

Mom placed the bowl of potato salad in the middle of the table and straightened. "Just what I said. It's felt strange not having him about the place like he used to be. So I figured the two of you needed a push to get you talking again." She smiled. "I guess it worked." Then she left me standing by the table, my mouth open, while she went to bring in the rest of the meal.

My mom was pretty amazing.

August 2005

AFTER LUNCH I went to the shower block to wash our plates, then dried them and brought them back to the large tent. Dad had insisted we bring it, saying that the small two-man tent was fine when we were kids, but not now. He had a point. We'd brought a lot more stuff than I'd anticipated, but most of it was because of Mom. You'd have thought we were going on an expedition with the amount of things she'd demanded we take with us.

The surprise had occurred just before we'd gotten into the truck so Dad could drive us to the lake. Mom peered into the back. "Now, are you boys sure you have everything you need?"

Matt snickered, and I rolled my eyes. "Mom, even if we'd forgotten something—which I don't believe for a second—Mendota County Park isn't even fifteen minutes away. We could find a pay phone and call you."

"No need for that." Dad came around from his side of the truck and held something out to me. "Take this."

I stared at the small silver Nokia cell phone. "Seriously?"

"We were going to give it to you for your birthday, but I figured you might have need of it this week. I've already programmed in our number."

"That is so cool." I grinned and waved it at Matt, who gave me an eye roll of his own.

"Okay, let's get you two over to the park." Dad peered at me intently. "Say goodbye to your mom."

Like he had to tell me. Mom held her arms wide for a hug.

I stepped into them and whispered, "It's a week. What are you gonna do when I go to college?"

Mom chuckled into my ear. "And what makes you think we're letting you go to college?" She stepped back and pushed my hair away from my eyes. "It's the longest you've ever been away from home."

Dad sighed. "Sarah, he's nearly seventeen. He has to leave your nest sometime."

I kissed Mom's cheek. "Do you want me to call you?" I brandished my new phone.

Mom nodded, and I saw her grow a little less tense. "Have fun, you two."

As Dad pulled away from the curb, he glanced at Matt and me and shook his head. "Women."

I kept my mouth shut. Matt was the one with all the experience when it came to girls, so I bowed to his superior knowledge. Girls never seemed to be all that into me.

Matt was still chuckling when my dad drove out of the park.

"You think *your* mom was bad? You should have seen mine."

Then the moment had arrived to put up the tent.

Okay, confession time. All those years I went camping with my parents? They were the ones who erected the tents. So there I was, trying to work out how all the poles fitted together. Hey, no laughing, this shit isn't easy! And Matt was no better. He remarked later that we might have fared better if we'd been drunk. Yeah, possibly.

It took us a while, but eventually we had the bones of the tent in place. Then all we had to do was add the rest of it, right? Okay, so it wasn't *quite* that easy, but eventually we were done.

I have to admit, having a campfire was nice. I wanted to cook over it, but no, Mr. Boring brought out the little stove. I'd had visions of wrapping potatoes in foil and putting them in the fire. Matt had given me A Look and said something about not wanting to eat food that was raw in the middle. See? B-o-r-i-n-g. I mean, where was the adventure in eating out of a can?

I exited the tent and scanned the area, but there was no sign of Matt. I walked out of the campground and headed for the water. Sure enough, Matt was sitting by the water's edge, looking out over the lake. I sat down next to him on the blanket he'd brought from the tent and admired the view.

"There's a shallow launch for boats and canoes," he told me, not taking his eyes off the water.

"Pity we don't have canoes, then." My dad had drawn the line at letting us take out a boat. Maybe he'd made a connection between my driving skill and the idea of letting me loose on the lake. Yeah, I wasn't a natural driver.

I gazed at the tranquil scene, but that wasn't what was at the forefront of my mind. "I've missed this," I said softly.

Matt turned to look at me, his brow furrowed. "The lake?"

I shook my head. "Spending time with my best friend." When that perplexed expression didn't change, I sighed. "This last year, I hardly saw you, except in class." It was on the tip of my tongue: *Since you got yourself a girlfriend.*

Matt snorted. "Excuse me, Mr. President of the Student Council, Mr. School Newspaper, Member of the Yearbook Committee, Photography Club, Captain of the Debate team? Did I miss anything? You had no time for me this year."

"Well, you had no time for me either," I retorted. This wasn't going the way I'd pictured it. I pushed out a sigh. "Sorry. I didn't mean to sound so… antagonistic."

"Me either." Matt's brow cleared. "Wanna go for a swim?"

I grinned. "Yeah, why not?" Anything was better than talking.

Within minutes we'd changed into our shorts and were headed for the beach. The water was warm at first, but as we swam out farther, I could feel pockets of cooler water beneath us. I turned onto my back and stared up into the startlingly blue sky, not a cloud in sight.

"This is great."

Matt swam beside me on his front, his chin out of the water. "Isn't it?"

It all seemed so far away: school, Cathy, the impending year with its decisions, college. And right then I was more than happy for it to be so.

The past was behind us; the future could wait. I was happy in the present.

SITTING BY the campfire was fast becoming my favorite occupation. I loved watching the flames dance and flicker, loved feeling their warmth on my skin and seeing Matt's face glow in their light.

"It's almost ten o'clock," Matt reminded me.

"Huh?" I'd been lost in the fire.

"The fire?" His expression was amused. "We have to put it out by ten, remember?"

"Oh, yeah, sure." I smiled. "But it's not ten yet. We have a little longer." To be truthful, so many questions were colliding in my head at that moment, and I'd been wondering if I was brave enough to give voice to some of them.

Matt gave me a satisfied smile. "See? We managed to feed ourselves and clean up without having to resort to calling our parents." I coughed, and he shook his head, chuckling. "Oh my God. You've called your mom, haven't you?"

"I *might* have called her when I went to the restroom earlier," I admitted. "But that was only because she sent me a text."

He laughed out loud. "Moms."

I couldn't hold back any longer. "So, do you think you and Cathy will go to the same college?"

Matt snorted. "That would be no. She's already figured out where she's applying, whereas I don't have a clue."

"But… you're close friends, right?"

Matt smiled, his gaze focused on the fire. "Yeah, we are. However, she's not my best friend. That was—and probably always will be—you." His eyes met mine. "I learned a new word this year. Symbiosis."

I thought for a minute, trying to connect that word with his relationship. Then the ball dropped. "Then... you and Cathy didn't...."

Matt's eyes widened. "God, no. That would be too much like.... Ew."

I was intrigued. "What's *ew*?"

Matt shuddered. "It'd be like dating my sister."

I stared at him. "You mean, like incest?"

Matt nodded vehemently. "See? *Ew!*"

So I'd gotten it all wrong. Matt and Cathy weren't all loved up. They were friends, just like he and I were friends. Then something he'd said struck me. "How can Cathy have it all figured out? I have no idea where I want to go to college, what I want to major in."

Matt smiled. "There's still time." He paused, biting his lip.

I knew that look. "What are you thinking of?"

He gave a casual shrug. "I *had* thought about going to college here in Madison."

"Really?"

Matt nodded. "I could stay at home, so it would be less expensive. I'd still need a part-time job, of course, and I'd have to work throughout the summer." Another smile. "But not this summer."

"Me neither. My mom told me to take this summer off."

Matt chuckled. "Mine too." He reached behind him and picked up the two bottles of pop that had probably gone flat and were way too warm, and handed one to me. He raised his. "Here's to moms and their bright ideas."

I clinked my bottle against his. "I'll drink to that." Then I caught voices and rose hastily to my feet. "Time's up."

Matt doused the fire with water, watching to make sure it had gone out. Then we lay back and stared up at the sky, where the stars were already beginning to shine.

NOTE

A FEW years ago, I ran into Cathy in a coffee shop in Madison. After a firm hug, we sat a while, reminiscing about high school. She said something about that time that has stayed with me ever since.

She told me how happy she'd been to have Matt around back then. Their friendship had meant everything to her. In fact, it had made her last two years of high school bearable. Then she told me I had no idea how horrible it had felt to be alone in a sea of people. She'd made the decision to be with Matt to break free of that cycle.

I guess we all make decisions to protect ourselves. After all, I was no different, was I?

And yeah, I knew exactly how that felt.

Chapter Eight

June, 2006

MATT TOOK a long drink from his bottle of beer and sighed. "This was a damn good idea."

"What was—a last weekend camping before graduation, or sneaking bottles of beer into the cooler?" I grinned. I had to admit, the beer tasted fantastic. Maybe it was the fact that we were sitting by the lake, the sun beating down, and the prospect of two whole days of doing nothing but relaxing that gave it an extra bite.

Matt opened his eyes wide. "I did not *sneak* them, as you so crudely put it. Dad gave them to me when I was packing my bag. All he said was, 'Don't let your momma know, and don't drive if you've been drinking.'"

I took a glance around us. "I'll add to that advice. Don't let anyone *spot* us drinking. And by anyone, I mean the park superintendent. I heard from Pete Myres that he and some of his friends got barred from coming here after the super found their trunk full of booze a couple months ago."

Matt snorted. "I have no sympathy. What did they expect when they all got drunk off their asses and went waterskiing in the nude in broad daylight? They were lucky he didn't call the cops. And I *still* don't understand why he didn't, to be honest."

I laughed. "Really? You didn't know that the super is Dylan LeVon's uncle? Yeah, imagine how *that* would've looked if it had got out."

Matt let out a long whistle. "Well, I'll be. Lucky bastards." Then he snorted again. "Although they *had* to have been drunk to go waterskiing naked in April. It was damn cold!" He gave a furtive glance around us and then raised his bottle. "Here's to the graduating class of 2006."

"I'll drink to that." I clinked bottles with him.

"And speaking of graduation…." Matt gave me a sideways look. "Is your speech all written and memorized yet, Mr. Valedictorian?"

I groaned. "I still don't know why it's gotta be me up there. When I think of all the guys they could have chosen."

"Like who? Troy, the captain of the football team? Granted, he looks great in his uniform, but hell, the boy can't rub two sentences together." Matt's eyes gleamed. "Guess they could've picked Terry Norton—if they wanted everyone to fall asleep before his speech was over. Y'know, that boy could make a fortune."

"He could?"

Matt nodded. "All he has to do is record himself reading aloud, burn it onto some CDs, then sell them as a cure for insomnia. Works for me every time. Five minutes of listening to him give a science report and I'm snoring and drooling over my desk." He cocked his head. "So that's a no on the speech?"

I sighed heavily. I'd sort of been waiting for inspiration to strike; only thus far there'd been nothing.

"Well, don't leave it until we're sitting there in our caps and gowns, they've given out all the prizes, and the principal is beckoning you onto the stage," Matt advised. "That would be cutting it a little close." He took another drink and gazed out over the lake. "Who knows when we'll get to do this again?"

I smiled. "You talk like we're never gonna see each other after graduation."

Matt shrugged. "It'll be different. We'll both be working this summer. You'll be in that coffee shop, and I'll be minding Paula now that Momma's working." His momma had gotten herself a cleaning job, and Matt had offered to look after his twelve-year-old sister. His face lit up. "Hey, did I tell you? Mom and Dad gave me something a few nights ago."

"What was that?"

"An ATM card. Seems they never touched all that money I earned mowing lawns. Dad opened up a bank account in my name, and they put every cent into it. Momma said it was for emergencies. She didn't want me going off to college and worrying about money."

I shook my head. "You've got good folks there."

His face glowed. "Yeah." He took another long drink of beer.

"Where's Cathy this weekend?"

Matt's smile slipped. "She's visiting her grandparents in Milwaukee."

I knew what that meant. Over the last year, I'd gotten to know Cathy real well. She was a sweet girl who was going through hard times right then. Her parents had announced they were getting a divorce, and the stress of it all had taken its toll on her. Matt told me she'd escape to Milwaukee when the atmosphere in her house got too much to bear. I could understand why she'd chosen not to stay in Wisconsin—Cathy was going to college in Atlanta.

"You two gonna keep in touch?"

Matt nodded. "She says she wants *your* number before she leaves for Atlanta."

"Mine?"

Matt regarded me warmly. "That surprises you?"

I thought about it. "I guess not." The three of us had gone to the movies on several occasions, and we'd hung out together at school. Some of our more low-minded classmates had found that highly amusing, and there'd been asshole comments about threesomes. I just gave them the finger, while Matt plain ignored them. It was Cathy I felt sorry for. She really was a quiet little thing.

I came back to our conversation. "We'll still get to see each other on the weekends."

"Will we?" Matt's forehead creased into a frown. "We don't know what demands college is gonna put on us. We'll have new friends, new interests…." Then his brow smoothed out. "At least there's the chance of running into you on campus." He grinned. "Go on, confess. You only applied to UW-Madison because I did, right?" He preened. "Can't keep away from me, can you?"

I looked around my chair for something to throw at him, but damn, there was nothing except my bottle of beer. "Smartass."

"Apparently not smart enough to be valedictorian," Matt flung back at me with a smile. "Want my advice about the speech?"

"Sure." Like I wasn't gonna ask him anyway.

Matt sat up and began counting off on his fingers. "Keep it short, like under eight minutes. Don't make it like those Oscar acceptance speeches that go on for hours."

"Got it."

"Do the usual 'what have we learned?' shit. Y'know, talk about how much we've all changed, how we've grown."

I chuckled. "Well, some of us have. I think Annabel Barrett is still about five feet nothing."

Matt nodded, smiling. "And that leads me to my next piece of advice. Make it funny. Not so that you have everyone rolling in the aisles, but yeah, a few laughs would be good. And then finish with a look to the future."

I sighed again. "It should be you up on that stage. You'd give a great speech."

Matt shook his head. "Nah. My job is to inspire you—and then sit in the front row and try to make you laugh the whole way through it."

I lunged for him, but before I could reach him, Matt was out of his chair and running toward the lake. "Last one in has to cook dinner!"

I gave chase. Damn it, it was his turn.

IT WAS a warm night, so once we'd put out the fire, we brought our sleeping bags out and lay on them, staring at the millions of stars above our heads.

"What you said earlier, about mentioning how we've all changed?"

"Hmm?" Matt inclined his head in my direction. "What about it?"

"Have we changed all that much?"

He pondered the question for a moment before answering. "I think so. I mean, I don't remember much about what you were like in second grade. You've always been smart, unafraid to voice your opinion."

I snorted. "Is that another way of saying I'm pigheaded? Overbearing?"

Matt chuckled. "For someone who loves words the way you do, you sure do choose the wrong ones sometimes. I'd have said assertive, uncompromising…."

"You mean cocky."

Matt rolled onto his side to face me, his head resting in his hand. "You've never been one for hiding your light under a bushel, as they say, and I know there've been some students who resented your consistent academic success, but…." He paused. "They also know that you don't back down in a fight. You stand up for what's right. You support the underdog." He smiled. "Like me."

I rolled onto my side, my body language mimicking his. "You were never the underdog."

"Ya think? I've had my share of people who thought it was okay to tease and bully me. Thing is, most of them learned pretty fast that if they tangled with me, they tangled with you too."

I smiled. "What are best friends for?" I watched him for a moment, recalling the ten years of our friendship. "Do you think we'll still be friends when we're older?"

Matt laughed. "We're already older, and getting older by the minute. And who knows what the future holds for us? College, jobs, careers… all those things will bring changes." He studied my face for a minute, so carefully that I was dying to ask what he was thinking. Then he smiled. "I *will* say this. I hope that whatever future awaits me has you in it."

I couldn't hold back my own smile. "Sounds good to me."

NOTE

MAYBE IT was because we were eighteen—and at that age you feel freaking immortal, right?—but in that moment, I truly believed Matt and I were going to be friends for the rest of our lives. Twelfth grade saw us reconnected, stronger than ever, and it taught me a couple of things. One, I'd never make assumptions again, because more often than not, those would be proved wrong. Cathy and Matt's friendship proved that. And two, my life was better with Matt in it, and I was going to hold on to that for as long as I could.

Graduation Day.

I STEPPED up to the podium and gazed out at the hall, packed to the rafters with students, their families, and friends. Behind me sat the teachers, the principal, and the vice principal. The front rows contained the graduating class, bedecked in our blue robes, some of the students clutching their prizes.

Matt hadn't managed to be on the front row, due to his surname, but I could see his beaming smile as he clutched his trophy. He'd received the school's math award, and the roar of applause that had greeted this announcement had plainly overcome him. Matt had no idea how popular he was, but his pleasure at hearing his classmates cheer for him was a joy to see. A few rows behind him, I caught sight of our parents, who'd sat together, and Matt's mom had tears streaming down her cheeks.

But finally it was my turn to speak, and my heart was pounding as I adjusted the mic, my eyes focused on a spot at the rear of the hall. Anywhere but Matt's grinning face, the bastard.

I took a deep breath. "Thank you all for coming here today to learn more about the fabulous opportunity that is Amway." When laughter broke out, I risked a glance in Matt's direction. He beamed at me, giving me the thumbs-up.

Yeah, I was gonna be just fine.

I thanked the teachers, the principal, the custodians—hell, I even thanked the janitor's kitty, that could often be seen strolling along the hall, proudly clutching between her jaws a freshly caught mouse. Okay, so that last part wasn't true—there were no pets allowed in school—but it sure raised a laugh. I harked back to how we'd entered high school as innocent freshmen, only to grow to our present status, the class who ruled the school. I spoke of our debt of gratitude to those who'd shaped our lives, from the principal down to the lunchroom attendants who put up with us slobs. I spoke of the support team that stood behind each graduate, and that the best way we could show our gratitude was by going out into the world and making it a better place. The adults in the room were nodding in approval.

Then I was ready for the finale.

"On a final note, I want to share with my fellow classmates some pearls of wisdom that I've picked up during my years here at Van Hise. Just some observations that might help you along life's highway." I paused. "Guys, we are *not* funnier than the girls. We just make more jokes. The thing is, we don't care sometimes whether other people share our sense of humor."

That got a few of the students blinking.

"I've learned that listening to high-volume music makes you feel calm, relaxed, and happy. We just need to make sure we do it with earplugs."

That caused a ripple of laughter.

"If you've done a lot of things you're ashamed of while growing up, don't be so quick to push away the guilt. It helps you to better understand other people's thoughts and feelings. And the people who give the best advice are usually the ones with the most problems." I gave them a moment to digest that one. "A word to the wise: the way a person treats a restaurant server says a lot about their character. And never judge a person by their handwriting. The smarter he is, the faster he thinks, and the sloppier he writes." I winked. "We only have to look at Mr. Trent to know that's true, right?"

More chuckles followed that. Mr. Trent's scrawl on the white board was legendary, but he had one of the finest minds in the school.

Matt was rolling his eyes.

"My last gem is this. They say that any friendship born in the period between sixteen and twenty-eight years of age is more likely to last longer, so look around you, guys. You're probably sitting with the best friends you'll ever have." My gaze flickered toward Matt, and I smiled. "Cherish them."

When the student body rose to their feet in applause, I took a bow and walked off the stage, content.

DAD RAISED his glass. "To our graduates, David and Matt."

My cheeks grew hot as everyone around the long table toasted us. Next to me, Matt couldn't stop smiling. I knew exactly how he felt. Our last day of high school, and it had been wonderful. But when we exited the hall and Dad told us we were all going to dinner at Naples 15, that was the icing on the cake. My favorite restaurant. Matt had never been there before, so all the way there I kept regaling him with tales of hot salami, and ricotta cheese and bacon pizza, chicken served in a cream sauce with roast bacon and smoked mozzarella, home-made ravioli filled with fresh lobster and covered in a white cream sauce, and ziti al Re di Napoli, a dish of pork and beef, slow-cooked to perfection in red wine. By the time I'd finished, he was drooling.

The food was amazing, and Matt kept dipping into everyone else's plates, sampling a little of everything. Judging by his blissful expression, he loved Naples 15 too. It was good to share the meal with his parents, and even his sister seemed to be enjoying herself, especially when the piano player began playing and several singers took turns with Italian folk songs.

When we were too stuffed to move—yeah, right, we were teenagers. Like that was gonna happen—the chef, Salvatore, appeared at our table, carrying a cake with lit candles. He congratulated us, and then the cake was shared.

Yeah, I found room for cake.

Of course, the magical night had to come to an end, and I walked out of the restaurant a happy, well-fed graduate. Matt was quiet, but I wasn't too concerned. A contented smile played about his lips. It was the perfect ending.

NOTE

I'VE LOST count of the number of times Matt and I have eaten in Naples 15 since that night, but that night sticks in my mind as the most special.

Well… nearly the most special.

Chapter Nine

December, 2006

I SCANNED the attic, searching for the boxes I knew were there somewhere. "Now I know why you haven't put up a tree yet," I yelled down to my mom. "You couldn't find the ornaments among all this shit." I shook my head. A week to go until Christmas and the house looked like Ebenezer Scrooge lived there—not a decoration in sight. When I got home from college for the holidays, I felt sure I'd driven to the wrong house. It stuck out like a sore thumb amid the brightly lit houses on that segment of South Segoe. Next door's lights were so numerous and so bright, it was like they wanted to be seen from space.

"Watch your mouth, mister. And most of that *shit*, as you so eloquently put it, is yours."

I muttered under my breath, something about being sure I hadn't left *this* much crap behind when I'd moved into my dorm in September. It had still been a shock to find my room as I'd left it. I was sure Mom would've have turned it into a sewing room or a place to do all her craft stuff, but no. And judging by how much stuff was still where I'd left it, I knew what she was claiming was a lot of BS.

I peered into the farthest corner of the attic and let loose a triumphant cry. "Found them." There had to be four or five large plastic crates filled to the brim, as well as a box containing what looked like a mass of snakes—the cables for the outdoor lights. Speaking of which….

"Hey, I don't see Frosty up here!"

Mom stuck her head through the attic door. "There's a reason for that. We had to retire him after last Christmas."

"You did what? I *loved* that snowman." Frosty had stood on our front lawn for as many holidays as I could remember, all lit up inside, with a jolly smile, a bright red scarf, and a tall black hat. Man, I'd charted my growth as a kid by comparing myself to that snowman.

Mom sighed. "David, come on. He had holes in him, he was that old. The only reason we kept him for so long was that you loved him." She shook her head. "Would you listen to me? I'm referring to a Christmas decoration as him." Her gaze met mine. "I blame you."

I huffed and took stock of my surroundings. "I thought you guys were going to finish the attic and turn it into something."

"Your dad did."

I blinked. "What did he turn it into? A dumping ground?" There were boxes everywhere—decorations for Christmas, Halloween, Thanksgiving…. Shit, was that Easter stuff? They were all shoved to one side of the attic, while the other held Dad's tools. Granted, most of them were old or broken, but he refused to throw them out in case he needed them.

Mom grimaced. "He turned it into a place where good things go to die." From her expression I guessed it was still a bone of contention between them. Then she confirmed my suspicions with a sigh. "Trust me, I've asked. I figure it's easier to just let him have his way." She straightened her features. "Now, bring down the boxes so we can make this place look festive."

From below I heard the doorbell ring. "That'll be Matt. I told him to come over."

Mom rolled her eyes. "How unexpected." Then she smiled. "What would this place be like without the other half of the Dynamic Duo? I'll go let him in." She arched her eyebrows. "Unless he has his own key by now?"

I gave her a mock scowl. "Funny lady. Jeez, I'm splitting my sides here."

Mom wagged her finger. "You may be in college, young man, but you are not too old for a spanking." She disappeared from view.

I laughed quietly to myself while I brought all the crates and accessories to the attic hatch, ready to take them down the steps. By the time I had them all in place, Matt popped his head through the space, grinning.

"Need a hand?"

"Perfect timing." I handed him the first of the crates, and between us we maneuvered them through the opening.

"Why are your folks so late in putting up the lights?" Matt whispered as I folded the steps up into the roof space and closed the hatch.

Before I could reply, Mom was there. "Because we thought we'd wait until David got home. It wouldn't feel like Christmas if he didn't decorate the house." She smiled at Matt. "Come to think of it, you've been part of that tradition for a few years now." Mom leaned over and gave him a peck on the cheek. "Good to have you here."

Matt gave one of those smiles of his that lit up his whole face. "Aw, thanks. I'm glad to be here."

"So, would you two boys like some hot chocolate while you sort through the crates? I imagine you have big, important tasks to do, such as making sure the lights work *before* they go up." Another grin and she left us to it.

"Was that your mom being sarcastic?"

I snorted. "No, that was my mom having a dig at my dad. One year he didn't check, and we only found out there was a problem after he'd covered the entire roof with lights." I gestured to one of the crates. "Give me a hand taking these into the living room. We can go through them there."

It wasn't long before we were sitting on the couch, drinking hot chocolate, and surveying the contents of the crates.

"Hey, Mom?" I hollered toward the kitchen. "Do you think we've got enough?"

She appeared in the doorway, hands on her hips. "David Stephen Lennon, if it were up to you, every inch of the outside of this house would be covered in lights, and the interior would look like a Christmas catalog. So yes, I think we have enough, and no, you are *not* going on a trip to the Home Depot to buy more. You got that?" She leveled a firm stare in my direction and then went back into the kitchen.

Matt chuckled. "I love it when your mom gets pissed and uses all your names." He sighed. "Okay, let's check that all the bulbs work; then we can start."

"We?" I arched my eyebrows.

Matt snorted. "What—you think I'm gonna let you have all the fun? Why d'you think I'm over here in the first place, to see *you*?" He rolled his eyes. "Gee, it's not like I didn't get to see much of you during the semester."

I shoved a bag of lights into his empty hands. "Get working, slave."

Matt shook his head, chuckling. For the next thirty minutes or so, we plugged in all the strands, replaced dead bulbs, and checked the fuse bulbs until we were satisfied everything was in working order.

"It was really nice of your parents to invite us all over for Christmas Day," Matt said softly. "Momma loves getting together with your mom." He smiled. "I see your mom sometimes when she comes over."

"Is it weird living at home?" Although I relished the freedom that living in a dorm afforded, there were times I wished I'd stayed at home too.

Matt shrugged. "Not really. My folks say I can move into a dorm house in my second year."

"Hey, that's great. We could be in the same house."

He laughed. "Like I didn't see that coming." Then his face clouded over.

I stilled instantly. "What's wrong?"

"Oh, it's nothing."

"Yeah, right." I studied him for a moment. "Come on, tell me. 'Cause you *know* I'm not gonna let up until you do."

He said nothing for a minute, and I felt sure he was about to tell me to drop it. Then he sighed. "Darren's home right now."

I knew Darren lived in Atlanta and came to visit his parents every couple of months or so. "Okay." I waited for the rest.

"Yeah, only this time he's brought his girlfriend with him. Gail."

"Is that a problem?" I frowned. "Don't you like her?"

Matt opened his eyes wide. "Gail? She's cool. Seriously, she's really sweet. You talk with her for ten minutes before you wonder what the hell she's doing with an asshole like Darren."

Ah-ha. "What's he said now?"

Matt huffed. "He started on me last night."

"About what?"

He gave a casual shrug that didn't fool me for a second. "Wanted to know if I'd gotten laid yet. Then he wanted to know if I was a 'fag.'" He air-quoted.

"What the hell?" I wanted to march right over to Matt's house and tear Darren a new asshole. "Dude, your private life is just that—private, and none of his fucking business." A thought occurred to me. "Darren's invited here too. Good." I was gonna make sure he left knowing exactly what I thought of the low-life piece of shit.

Matt shook his head violently. "You can't say a word. Gail will be here too."

I set my jaw. "Then she needs to know what he's really like. God, it was bad enough when we were in eleventh grade." I burned with outrage. Even *I* didn't ask stuff like that, because it had nothing to do with me. I'd learned my lesson with the whole Cathy situation.

Matt laid a hand on my arm. "David? Leave it, please." His gaze met mine. "Do it for me. For a peaceful Christmas. Whatever. Just… don't say anything, okay?"

My rage slipped from boiling to a simmer. "Okay," I agreed grudgingly. "But if he says one word—"

"He won't. Darren's not stupid. He knows he'd be in real shit with my folks if he did that." Matt sighed. "He wasn't always like this. Maybe it's stuff he picked up from college." He stared pointedly at me. "But if *I* can ignore him, I'm damn sure *you* can."

I was about to say that it was obvious from his face that he wasn't ignoring it, but then Dad came into the living room.

"Ah, time to decorate for the holidays." He jerked his head to one side. "Did you see all the lights on Terry Mason's place? There have to be at least a billion light bulbs."

"I think it's neat," Matt said. "But I'm sure yours will look just as good."

"Well, I don't know." Dad glanced toward the kitchen. "I told your mom that we could have a change this year. She wasn't too keen on my suggestion, however."

"Why, what did you suggest?" I thought my mom loved all the lights.

"I said we could take a strand of white lights and arrange them in the living room window to read 'Ditto,' with an arrow pointing toward Terry's place."

I snickered. "I can see why she wouldn't be too keen on that."

Dad tossed me the keys to his truck. "How about you and Matt go over to Tree City and pick us out a tree?"

I stared at the keys. "Really?" That was always something Dad did. I just went along for the ride and to argue about how the tree he'd chosen was too small. I mean, every freaking time.

Dad chuckled. "Yeah, well, I thought maybe this year we'd cut out the high-level discussions about the correct height for a Christmas tree and just let you get on with it." He winked at Matt. "Anything for a quiet life. Just keep in mind where you're going to put it." He pointed toward the ceiling. "I have no plans to cut a hole in *that*, just to accommodate your ten-foot-high tree."

I snorted and grabbed my jacket and scarf. "Ten feet." I waited until Matt and I had reached the door. "I was thinking at least twelve." I fled, laughing, as a cushion sailed across the room and smacked into the door.

"WE NEED to choose one, Matt." We'd already walked around Tree City three times, and it didn't feel like we were any nearer to making a decision. I was starting to get cold, pulling my thick jacket tightly around me.

"But how? They all look great."

"Does it always take this long to choose a tree in your house?" I grinned.

Matt shrugged. "I wouldn't know. We've never had a real one. There was always this artificial tree that's been around as long as I can remember. Dad used to say, why buy a tree that you're gonna throw out at New Year? He said it was a waste of money." Matt's wistful expression told another story, however.

That did it. Matt was going to choose the tree this year.

"Okay, then let's make this a process of elimination." I grabbed hold of his elbow and steered him toward the section containing the white pines. "What about these?"

Matt shook his head. "They're too… fluffy-looking."

I gaped. "Fluffy-looking?" I gazed at the trees, with their masses of long needles. Okay, maybe he had a point. "Fine. No white pines, then." I dragged him over to the scotch pines. "And how about these? They've got a great shape." That perfect conical Christmas tree shape.

"True." Matt leaned in and sniffed. "But they don't *smell* like a Christmas tree. They should have a scent that fills the room."

Now we were getting somewhere. "I think I have the answer." I took him to the section containing the balsam firs and flung out my arm toward them. "There."

Matt sniffed, and a wonderful smile lit up his face. "Oh, that's beautiful. And it's so bushy."

The guy in the Tree City jacket who was standing nearby nodded. "Gotta make sure you keep it watered if you wanna keep them needles. But it'll keep its smell all through Christmas and well into the new year."

Matt was nodding too, his eyes shining. "One of these."

We spent fifteen minutes pulling out and examining trees, until the guy gave up on us and went to help another customer. Then Matt spied a tree in the corner. "That one."

I estimated it to be about eight feet tall. "My dad will pitch a fit if we take that home. Plus we'll never get the angel to sit on top of it."

Matt stepped back and peered at the base. "Then we take a chunk off the bottom of the trunk. There's room for that."

The guy in the jacket was back. "That's what you should always do with a tree anyhow. Makes it easier to take up water."

Matt was smiling. "See? This one. It's perfect."

I had to agree, it was a beautiful tree. I think the guy was relieved we'd come to a decision.

Once I'd paid for it, he hefted it onto his shoulder. "I'll take it to your vehicle."

We led him to the truck, and he placed it in the back with surprising care. "You have to be careful," he told us. "Them needles break real easy." He smiled at us. "You guys will love it in your place. Happy holidays." And with that he walked off.

Matt's mouth fell open. "Er, David? He thought we were together. You know, a couple."

I snorted. "In which case he was more laid-back than your brother. Good for him." I winked. "Shall we take *our* tree home, *dear*?"

Yeah, I totally expected that whack on the arm.

BY THE time we'd finished, the house looked amazing. Blue lights festooned the windows, dripping down the panes like icicles. Garlands covered the mantel over the fireplace and the tops of the doors. But the tree was our masterpiece.

Matt had had the idea of taking every set of tiny white lights we could find and covered the tree with them, making sure to light up the inside too. Then we'd set about hanging the baubles. There were decorations that dated back to the fifties, ornaments given to my parents by my grandparents, and the ones that had marked off every year since I'd been born. Each year Mom had bought a new ornament, and I laid those out on the coffee table for Matt.

"This is so neat." He pointed to a little glass cottage already hanging from a branch. "It seems so… fragile."

I smiled. "That one is German, and it's very old."

Mom came into the living room and smiled when she saw the table. "Ah, I'm just in time." She handed us each a small white box and then stood there, clearly waiting.

"What's this?" I opened the box and let out a sigh. "Oh, Mom." It was a small ceramic Christmas wreath with a little boy in the middle of it. Above on a banner were the words UW-Madison, and below was my name. "This is great." I glanced over at Matt and saw his was similar to mine.

Matt's eyes glistened. "You bought a tree ornament… for me?"

Mom's eyes were suspiciously shiny. "Well, you've been around this family for over ten years, Matt. I figured it was time you had your own ornament." Her voice cracked slightly.

Matt placed the wreath back into its box almost reverently, and then he lurched to his feet and flung his arms around my mom. She stiffened in surprise but quickly relaxed and hugged him back.

"Merry Christmas, Matt."

"Thank you," he whispered. When he released her, he smiled and cleared his throat. "Okay. I need to hang this."

We found two branches where there was a bare spot, and we hung the wreaths next to each other.

"There." Mom beamed. "Together as always." She went into the kitchen with the excuse of pouring us some eggnog, but I wasn't fooled.

Matt gazed at the tree, his eyes wide. "I think this gets close to being the best holiday ever."

"And we haven't even had Christmas Day yet," I added.

Matt turned to me and smiled. "Then it can only get better."

Christmas Day

"SARAH, CAN I do anything to help?" Matt's mom asked as we cleared away the dishes from the extended dining table.

Mom smiled. "You could help me with the coffee." She gave a nod to me. "And when you've loaded the dishwasher, you and Matt can see if anyone wants anything else to eat."

I groaned. "After that meal? Even *I* couldn't manage another bite."

"And that's really saying something," Matt added with a sly wink.

"Hey!" I smacked him on the arm.

"Not while you're carrying my best china, you don't." Mom's eyes flashed.

Sheepishly, I carried the plates through to the kitchen and set about my task. Once the racks had been filled, I went into the living room, where Matt was already circulating, a box of mints in one hand and chocolates in the other. Unsurprisingly there were few takers.

My dad and Matt's were discussing the new head coach for the Wisconsin Badgers football team and bemoaning Barry Alvarez's resignation. I glanced across at Matt and rolled my eyes. He chuckled. Neither of us were all that into football.

Matt's sister, Paula, was ignoring us, her nose stuck in a book she'd gotten for Christmas. Matt shook his head and mouthed, *Teenager.* I tried not to laugh. I'd been the same at her age.

"Your mom is a great cook." Gail settled back against the cushions on the couch, Darren beside her. "That was amazing. There was so much food."

I laughed. "I think Mom's rule of thumb is to look at how many guests she's expecting and provide food for twice that number." Matt had been correct; I liked her. She had long blonde hair, pretty blue eyes, and a sweet smile. I loved her Southern drawl. It reminded me a little of how Matt had first sounded when we met.

Totally too good for Darren, in my opinion.

"How long have you two been dating?" I asked her, perching on the arm of the couch.

"Since the spring." She flicked a glance in Darren's direction. "We met when Darren joined the software company where I work." She gave a shy smile. "You know people talk about meeting up and having conversations around the water cooler? Well, we got talking one day, and it seemed like next to no time before he was asking me out. When he asked me to come spend the holidays with him and his family, I thought it was a great idea."

"Don't you be fooled by the 'butter wouldn't melt' exterior," Matt joked. "Gail's a card shark." He winked at me.

She gasped. "I am *not*. Beating the pants off you at UNO does *not* make me a cheat."

I snickered. "UNO, huh?" I left her giggling and went over to Matt, who was standing beside the tree. I leaned in close. "Yep. I like her." I also liked how she and Matt had already gotten close. He seemed really at ease with her.

Mom bustled in from the kitchen with a tray full of coffee cups, Matt's mom following with the pot, sugar bowl, and cream. "David, I think it's time to hand out some presents, don't you?"

I nodded. There were gifts under the tree for Matt's family, just little presents as a reminder of the day. I handed them around and then dashed from the living room to grab Matt's present from my room. As I reentered the living room, however, I caught low cries and cheers.

"What's going on?"

Matt laughed. "See what happens when you leave at just the wrong moment?" He pointed to where Darren was kneeling in front of Gail, her left hand clasped in his. Matt beamed. "Looks like I'm gonna have a sister-in-law."

Gail's face was flushed and happy, and her gaze flitted between Darren and the sparkling ring on her finger. Judging by the astonishment etched across Matt's parents' faces, they'd had no idea.

Gail got up from the couch to receive hugs of congratulations from everyone, and Darren shook hands with his dad and mine. He looked across at Matt. "When the time comes, will you stand with me?"

Matt blinked. "Seriously?"

I could understand his shock. Darren had never given the impression of being overly fond of him.

Darren snickered. "Well, duh. You *are* my brother. Who else am I gonna ask? Besides, I wouldn't trust those jackasses I work with to be able to organize my bachelor party." He winked. "I'd probably end up arrested."

"Okay, sure." Matt grinned. "As long as you know I'm not one for being predictable."

Darren's gaze flickered in my direction for a second, and then he grinned back. "I think I'll cope." He went back to receiving hugs from his mom. Gail still looked thunderstruck.

I took the opportunity to hand Matt his gift. "Merry Christmas."

He didn't bat an eyelid, but instead reached into his pants pocket and removed a small wrapped package. "Merry Christmas. It's not much, but…."

I shook my head. "Have you never heard 'it's the thought that counts'?" I tore away the paper, opened the box, and—

My jaw dropped. "Star Trek insignia? This is so cool." Then I really looked at it, and gasped. "You made me a captain. Dude."

Matt did an eye roll. "To quote my erudite brother—Well, duh." He grinned. "My turn." He tore into the soft package, unfolded its contents, and started laughing. "Oh, that's great." He held the T-shirt against his chest. "Mom, Dad? Look what David bought me for Christmas."

His dad peered closely and read aloud the words on the front. "Four out of three people struggle with math." He grinned. "God, he really knows you, doesn't he?"

Matt laughed, and his gaze met mine. "Of course he does." His eyes shone. "He's my best friend."

NOTE

I ALWAYS loved the holidays, but Christmas of 2006 has to be one of my favorites. It was a time for family. Gail told me years later that it was that day when she realized she'd not only gained a brother-in-law-to-be, but she'd also gained an extra brother—me—because Matt and I were "sort of a package deal," as she put it.

Yep. That sounded right.

Chapter Ten

July, 2007

I WAS trying hard not to laugh. Matt noticed, of course. Like he ever missed anything I did. "What's so amusing?"

"Your brother's expression, that's what. You can almost read his mind from here." I opened my eyes wide. "My little brother organized my bachelor party... in a *bowling alley*?"

Matt chuckled. "You should've heard him when I first told him. His eyes bugged out like he thought I'd gone crazy." He shrugged. "I told him it would be laid-back and a lotta fun."

All the guys in the five lanes behind me certainly seemed to be having fun. The tables were covered with snacks and beer, and the air was alive with competitive spirit. Not everyone was bowling. Some were sitting around, talking, and laughing.

Pity Darren wasn't one of them.

"He really needs to loosen up." I risked another glance in his direction and froze. "Oh God, he's coming this way."

Matt smothered another chuckle and did his best to straighten his face. By the time Darren reached us, he'd almost managed it.

Almost.

"Hey, having a good time?" he asked Darren innocently.

Darren stared at him. "Bowl-A-Vard? You had to be different, huh? You couldn't do something normal, you know, like book us a bar, with music and strippers?" He flung his arm out toward the bowling lanes. "A fifties-style bowling alley?"

Matt bit his lip. "I thought you loved *Happy Days*."

Darren's eyes bulged. "When I was a kid, sure! I mean, who *didn't* love the Fonz? But now?" He shook his head. "You screwed up."

"Aw, don't be so hard on him," I interjected. "The party's only just got going. Besides, he could have organized it on bike night." I knew my lips were twitching, but I couldn't help it.

Darren regarded me with a baleful stare. "Bike night," he said heavily. "That would at least have been preferable to tons of little kids running around." He gazed out at the guys who'd turned up so far. "What must they be thinking?"

"Actually?" Matt smiled. "Several guys have come over to say how great this is… and to ask why you're being such a dick." He didn't break eye contact.

Darren opened his mouth, then snapped it shut. He blinked, then sighed. "Sorry, Matt. I shouldn't take out my bad mood on you. Especially after you went to all this trouble."

This was so atypical of Darren that I was blinking too.

"Er, okay." Judging by Matt's expression, he was equally surprised by this new Darren. He regarded Darren closely. "Hey, what's wrong? You should be over the moon. You're getting married in a week."

"Yeah, well, I sorta messed up." Darren's face flushed. "You see those two guys over there?" He inclined his head toward the farthest lane, where two men sat watching the bowling.

Matt gazed at them for a second. "Sure. Who are they?"

"Well, the guy on the left is Gail's uncle, Roy. The guy next to him is his… partner."

Matt stilled. "As in… partner, partner?"

I peered in their direction. They looked like they were in their forties. They were talking quietly and smiling, drinking beer, and observing the antics of the younger guys.

Darren sighed. "When Gail and I were writing the wedding invitations, I asked why I was sending one to two guys. When she told me they were her uncle and his… other half, I… made a comment. And… I might have called them a name that she didn't like much."

"I can guess what," I commented dryly.

Instead of glaring at me like I'd expected, Darren nodded gloomily. "Gail was super pissed. She gave me a lecture on how I should be ashamed of myself, that it didn't matter if they're… gay. Then I ended up in the doghouse for a week."

I smirked. I assumed that was Darren-speak for Gail kicking him out of bed. From Matt's expression, he'd arrived at the same conclusion.

"You don't exactly have a good track record when it comes to LGBT acceptance, do you?" Matt said quietly. "So what did you say to her that got you out of trouble?"

"I said... I didn't hate gay people," Darren muttered.

Matt raised his eyebrows.

"And... I also said I would try to be... better."

"What was her response?"

Darren expelled a long breath. "She insisted if I got to know her... uncles, I'd like them."

Matt shook his head. "You do know if she has to keep reading you the riot act, that will piss her off even more? Not exactly the basis for a happy marriage."

"Yeah, I know."

"This might sound like a strange question," I ventured, "but do you actually *know* anyone who's gay?"

Darren opened and closed his mouth. "Uh, no. That I know of," he amended hastily.

"Then maybe you should wander over there and introduce yourself to them," Matt suggested. He flashed Darren a smile. "You might find out they're as normal as you."

"And when you've done that, it might be a good idea to go talk to your guests and maybe do some bowling?" I grinned. "You might even have fun."

"Yeah, you're right." Darren sighed. He regarded Matt with an amused expression. "I guess my little brother grew up okay after all."

Matt bit his lip. "I think that was a compliment."

Darren laughed and patted him on the back before heading over to where Gail's uncles sat.

"Well, that was unexpected." I stared after him, watching as the three men engaged in conversation. When the couple smiled and nodded, I figured Darren was doing just fine.

Matt shook his head. "Maybe I should have organized that stripper after all."

"What stripper?"

Matt's eyes gleamed. "His name was Adam."

Oh my God. "You were gonna hire a *male* stripper? For Darren's bachelor party?" I had to give it to Matt, the guy had balls. Of course, he wouldn't have had them for long, once Darren had picked his jaw up off the floor and got his breath back.

Matt shrugged. "Call it payback for all the shit he's given me over the years. He's just lucky that I'm a nice guy."

"Then he got better than he deserved." I glanced over to where Darren was now chatting animatedly with more of the guys. "I think Gail will be good for him."

"I'd better make sure there's enough beer and snacks." Matt poked his finger at my chest. "And you're helping."

I raised my eyebrows. "Bossy little shit, aren't you?"

Matt was still giggling as I followed him into the bar.

THE CHURCH was full of flowers, and their perfume pervaded the air. All the guests were talking in hushed voices, everyone waiting for the bride's entrance. Matt stood at the front with Darren, who kept touching his cravat and gazing toward the rear of the church.

I got the distinct impression the bridegroom was nervous. Matt glanced across to where I sat in the second row from the front, and rolled his eyes. I'd never seen him in a suit before, and he looked really good. Then his attention was claimed by Darren once more.

"Will you stop doing that?" he murmured. "One, you look fine. Two, she'll be here, because God help her, she loves you."

Darren stilled, his face breaking into a smile. "Yeah, she does, doesn't she?"

I wanted to laugh. Gail had to be some kind of a miracle worker.

Then the music started up, and all heads turned to watch the doors as Gail entered, her face hidden by lace, her arm through her dad's.

"Oh, she's lovely," my mom whispered next to me, a tissue already clutched in her hand. In the front row, Matt's mom was staring at Gail, already misty-eyed.

Darren gazed at Gail with an expression of awe that made my stomach clench. It was like nothing existed for him in that moment but her. My heart ached to know that kind of love, and laced through it was a pang of regret. I wanted someone to look at *me* the way Darren looked at Gail, like she was *it* for him, pure and simple.

Across the aisle from me were rows of Gail's family, and behind them, her friends. In the second row sat her uncles, Roy and Michael, their gaze focused on Gail, both of them smiling. It wasn't until I glanced down that I noticed their hands were clasped together. Then I saw their matching rings.

Oh wow. At first I thought it brave of them to hold hands so publicly—you never knew when there was an asshole nearby—but then I reconsidered. If they couldn't hold hands in a church during a ceremony of love and commitment, then something was really wrong with the world.

Gail reached Darren's side, and I had to smile when he lifted her veil and beamed at her. Then I watched and listened while they made their vows, speaking softly to each other, like no one else was there. Now and then, Matt glanced at me, a smile in place the whole time.

NOTE

WHEN I was a kid, I hated going to weddings. Stuffy, uncomfortable affairs that bored me to tears. Events where I longed to kick off my stiff, unwieldy shoes and hot, itchy jacket. Receptions where I'd hide under the long tablecloths and sneak a hand out every now and then in search of cake.

But Darren and Gail's wedding marked a change in my perceptions.

Maybe it was my age. Maybe because I knew the participants. Maybe a combination of things. All I know is that love filled that small church, and for the first time in my life, I regretted that I'd never tasted its sweetness, never known its pleasures and pains. And whereas it had never figured all that prominently in my thoughts before that day, a shift had taken place inside me.

I wanted to feel what Darren and Gail so obviously felt.

I wanted to know love.

Of course, the ever-practical side of my brain got in on the act, arguing that I was only in my first year of college, for God's sake. There was plenty of time for love later.

Sure. Fine.

But at least I'd acknowledged that part of me—maybe only a tiny part, but still there—yearned to know what love was like.

"WELL, *THAT* is something I've never seen before." Matt's mom stood beside me as we watched the couples dancing to the gentle sways of the band. She held out her hand, containing a glass of champagne, in the direction of the dance floor, where Gail's Uncle Ray was dancing with his... husband? Their cheeks were pressed together, and Michael's eyes were closed, like he knew Ray wouldn't let him put a foot wrong.

I gazed at the other onlookers, curious to see their reactions. No one batted an eyelid. Well, almost no one—there was one couple who looked like they were sucking on a whole basket of lemons. Well, it sucked to be them. (Hey, see what I did there? Ha!)

"What—two men dancing together?" I said, half jokingly.

"They're wearing wedding bands," she whispered. "I think it's sweet," she added with a smile. "I wonder how long they've been together."

"I have no idea."

"Here, your hand is empty." Matt was at my side, holding out a glass of champagne. When his mom arched her eyebrows, he grinned. "Hey, it's a wedding. And I didn't ask for it—a nice server gave it to me." He gave her a beseeching look. "Aw, come on."

His mom laughed. "You must think I've really naïve. Did you think I didn't know about all those beers you used to take with you when you two went camping?" She rolled her eyes.

I took the glass. "Thanks. We were just discussing Roy and Michael."

"Ah. I was talking to Gail about them just now." Matt looked out to the dance floor where the couple were still circling, like they were lost in their own little world. "Seems they met in college, and they've been together ever since. Last year they went to Boston to get married, because it's legal there." He took a sip of champagne. "I think they're really brave. I mean, look around. They're the only gay couple in the room. That takes balls." His mom cleared her throat, and Matt coughed. "Sorry, Momma."

I caught sight of Darren, who was leading Gail onto the dance floor again. She'd removed the veil and was wearing flowers in her hair. "I think it was a wonderful wedding."

Matt's mom was watching them too. "I'm so happy to see Darren settled. He *is* twenty-five, after all."

I chuckled. "Yeah, I can see why you'd be concerned. That's ancient."

She gave me a hard stare, but I wasn't worried. We knew each other well by that point. She glanced at Matt. "That'll be you, one day."

"Just as long as you don't expect *me* to want to get married any day soon." Matt gave her one of those face-alighting smiles of his, his eyes gleaming.

His mom laughed. "Sweetheart, you've just started in college. Right now your studies are what matters most. You have plenty of time to meet the right girl. Wait until you're twenty." She looked across to the bar and smiled. "And now I'm going to grab your daddy and drag him onto the dance floor." She winked at us. "Whether he wants to or not."

I laughed as she walked purposefully over to Matt's dad, who watched her approach with mock trepidation. "Run, Daniel," I muttered under my breath. "Flee for your life." I liked that his parents had such a good relationship, after nearly thirty years of marriage.

Matt snorted. "He'll dance with her. Like he would miss an opportunity to put a smile on her face." Then he gaped. "Hey, it's just hit me. That remark about waiting till I'm twenty? She wasn't joking."

I burst into laughter. "You'd better start looking now, then."

Matt took a long drink of champagne, then shook his head. "I'm in no hurry. She can wait."

I knew the feeling. Marriage seemed like a distant spot on the horizon, but one that I now acknowledged. Because somewhere out there was someone who would fit me perfectly.

Someone who would love me.

NOTE

LOOKING BACK, I remember exactly what I felt at that moment when Matt spoke of getting married, and, I'm ashamed to admit, it was a pang of jealousy. Someday a girl would waltz into Matt's life. It would be just like it had been with Cathy, only this time it would be for real. He'd have fallen in love with her. Our friendship would undergo another change, only this one could very well be irrevocable. It was stupid, I know, but he was an important part of my life, and the thought of losing him—again—caused an ache in my heart.

Of course, at the time I quickly dismissed such thoughts, but they didn't go away entirely.

Chapter Eleven

August, 2009

COLLEGE WAS sort of a mixed experience for me. The academic side was great, and I pushed myself hard to maintain my own high standards, but as for the social aspect? That proved more of a challenge, even after three years. I suppose people really don't change all that much. I still found it difficult to make friends, and I guess part of that was the other students who didn't like my consistent academic success.

Thank God for Matt. I'm not sure if I'd have coped without having him around.

In 2007 at the beginning of our second year in college, Matt finally made the move to Dejope Residence Hall, which was right on Lake Mendota. In fact, we could see the lake from our window. Of course, his mom had gotten a little misty-eyed when I'd turned up with my dad's truck to help him move all his stuff. I guess it felt like he was finally leaving home, even if we weren't all that far away.

Our room was great. It sort of looked L-shaped, only that was because they'd put up a wall between the beds and the storage area. We had open closets with lots of hanger space, plus shelves and room under them. More shelves for food and—the best—a microwave oven. Shelves for books. Then around the corner into the other part of the room, and there was the window with another small bookcase below it, and a desk on either side.

The beds were single, a lofted bed above the other at right angles to it, and below it was another low bookcase with our TV, DVD player, and stereo on it. Matt had grabbed the lower bed and had strung up a couple of strands of tiny white lights from the base of my bed. We even had a couple of beanbag chairs for when we watched TV. I'd been concerned at first—I'd never shared a room before—but I needn't have worried. After a week or so, it felt totally normal.

Of course, we had to get used to each other's habits, not to mention each other's taste in movie posters, which changed with each year. You can guess what mine were, right? *Star Wars*, *Star Trek*, *Dune*…. Matt's were more… eclectic. *Beetlejuice*, *Jaws*, *Legend*, *Pirates of the Caribbean*, and *Alien vs Predator*. Yeah, diverse, right? As for habits…. Let's just say I weaned Matt off his habit of leaving the cap off the toothpaste, and he made sure I did the laundry more regularly.

When summer came and it was time to move out of our room and back home, I was kinda sad. I was going to miss Matt, especially since I was going to be working all summer. Which was all down to him, by the way.

Back in the fall of 2007, not long after we'd moved into the Hall, Matt came dashing into our room, clutching a piece of paper. "Hey! I just saw this on the bulletin board, so I stole it."

I laughed. "I'm afraid to ask."

He brandished the sheet in front of my eyes. "The University Book Store is advertising. Weekend jobs." When I said nothing, Matt rolled his eyes. "Oh, come on. You, working in a bookstore? Surely that has to be the Perfect Job for you? Surrounded by books all day, the air rich with that new book smell?"

When he put it like that….

So yeah, that was how I came to be working at the bookstore, and as I'd already mentioned, I worked there throughout the summer too. Matt got a job as a server in a restaurant that summer, so we didn't see much of each other. To be truthful, as much as I loved the summer months, I couldn't wait for fall for classes to start again.

So, back to August 2009 and the end of our third year. We'd moved out of the hall and back home. There were times when I found it hard to believe that we only had one year before graduation. Where did the time go? I was working in the bookstore, and Matt had gotten an office job working for Pepsi-Cola. He said it was okay, the pay was reasonable, but the best part was the hours—he started at nine and finished at two thirty, Tuesday to Saturday, which left his afternoons and Sunday free.

It was a beautiful July day, and every time I was near the store window, I glanced out at the blue sky, trying not to think about swimming in the lake, taking out a canoe, or simply lying on a towel, enjoying the sun. Then it was back to my task of putting out the new stock and checking that the shelves were all full.

"Excuse me, I'm looking for a book on the care and upkeep of Wisconsin painted turtles" came a funny voice from behind me.

I turned around, already knowing exactly who had spoken.

Matt grinned at me.

I sighed dramatically. "In all these years, you've never gotten any funnier, you know that?"

Matt widened his eyes and let out a short gasp. "I have a great sense of humor. It's not *my* fault that you don't share it." Then he smiled, the skin crinkling around his eyes. "*Some* of us have finished work for the day."

I made sure the store manager wasn't in sight before flipping Matt the bird. "You're a bastard. I have two more hours to go."

"Which is why I'm here, to provide light at the end of your tunnel. Wanna grab a burger and a movie tonight? I thought I'd meet you here and we could head straight for Dotty's. I've already checked out what's on at the Marquee." Dotty Dumpling's Dowry was our favorite burger joint.

"Fine, but I get to choose the movie."

Matt scowled. "Hey, you chose last time, remember? You made me sit through *Harry Potter and the Half Blood Prince*."

I caught my breath in mock horror. "*Made* you? What was so awful about seeing a Harry Potter movie? I mean, they're—"

"Yeah, yeah, we've already had this discussion." Matt waved a hand dismissively. "But it's *still* my turn." He stuck out his chin.

"Fine. What do you want to see?"

His eyes gleamed. "They're showing *Twilight* again."

"No. No." I lowered my voice. "No fucking *way*. I am *not* sitting through sparkly vampires again. It was bad enough when you dragged me to it the first *three* times."

Matt blinked innocently. "What was so bad about it?" His lips twitched.

"You mean, apart from the fact that we were surrounded by girls who screamed every time Taylor Lautner showed up on the screen? Or maybe the girls holding up banners with hashtag Team Edward and hashtag Team Jacob? Or—"

"Okay, fair enough. No *Twilight*." That gleam was still there, however. "What about… *500 Days of Summer*?"

I speared him with a look. "You mention another chick flick and you lose a testicle."

Matt let out an exaggerated sigh. "O-*kay. Aliens in the Attic*."

I could live with that. "You're on. Now fuck off out of here before my manager comes over to ask me why I'm not working."

Matt pouted. "Hey, I'm a customer. I still want my book on Wisconsin painted turtles."

"I'll buy it for you for Christmas. Now get out of here and I'll see you at five."

"Done." Matt smiled and walked away.

I shook my head. Yeah, thank God for Matt.

NOTE

THAT PART about Matt leaving the cap off the toothpaste?

Yeah, I might have been a little economical with the truth there. I mean, yes, he *did* do that, but he faced more of a challenge with me. Our three years of sharing a room could have been subtitled: When David Discovered His Inner Slob.

And I only got worse as I got older.

Again, thank God for Matt. Coping with my habits turned out to be one of his superpowers.

MATT CAME back from the restroom just as our server left the table. Matt gazed after him as he sat facing me. "You ordered already?"

"Uh-huh." I shoved the menu card back into its holder.

Matt frowned. "Why didn't you wait for me? How do you know what I want to eat?"

I did an eye roll. "Please. Like I don't know you by now." I counted off on my fingers. "Cock 'n' Bull ginger beer, Heart Throb burger with sides of onion rings, sweet potato fries, and deep fried pickles." I flashed him what I hoped was a smug grin. "Happy now?"

Matt gave a little contented sigh and settled against the chair back. "Okay, you're off the hook." He smacked his lips. "I love their Heart Throb sauce."

"You can keep it." I wasn't that keen on jalapeños and cilantro. "I'm having a root beer, the Melting Pot burger, and poutine fries."

Matt laughed. "You and your cheese curds. Easy to tell you were born here." He let out another satisfied sigh. "I love Dotty's burgers."

I pointed to the sign above the bar. "Well, we *are* in the World Hamburger Headquarters, after all." I grinned. Ever since he'd appeared in the bookstore, I'd been looking forward to this. Well, not so much the movie—initial reviews suggested it might be the recipient of a Raspberry Award—but the idea of chilling out with Matt over a burger was very pleasant.

When the server brought over our beverages, I took a long drink of my root beer, relishing the icy-cold liquid sliding down my throat. "So, anything new I need to be updated on?" Matt always made me laugh with his stories about his coworkers.

Matt regarded me for a second before reaching for his ginger beer and hastily swallowing a mouthful. "You know, it's funny you should ask that…." Another quick drink. "I got asked out today."

I paused, the glass midway to my mouth. "Asked out… on a date?"

Matt nodded. "One of the interns, Sandra, asked if I'd like to go to a party with her."

I arched my eyebrows. "You haven't mentioned her before."

He gave a quick shrug. "We talk during the lunch break sometimes. She's okay."

"Only okay? Your enthusiasm is underwhelming." I was surprised. Matt hadn't gone on a date since Cathy.

Matt chuckled. "It shows, huh? Don't get me wrong, she's kinda sweet, but I sorta got the impression that I was part of a plan."

"What do you mean?"

"She really likes Terry, one of the technicians—I see her staring at him all the time—but so far he hasn't noticed her. I figure she asked me to see what he'd do." He laughed. "Seeing as she asked me when he was standing right by us. Really subtle, huh?"

"Ah-ha, a strategic proposal. Did it work?"

Matt grinned. "Like a charm. I refused politely, she pouted, and Terry stepped up to be the hero."

"Still, you could have gone with her."

Matt stared at me. "Sure. I could have stood around with a bunch of people I didn't know, made enough small talk to drive me to drink, and snuck glances at my phone until a decent interval had passed before I could make an excuse and leave. Or, I could spend the evening eating my favorite burger before sitting next to you in a movie theater and making inane comments to bug you." Another grin. "Sounds like a no-brainer to me."

"Well, when you put it like that." I raised my glass. "To Sandra and Terry. May their evening bring them all they desire."

"I'll drink to that." Matt clinked his glass to mine. "Besides, I get to slap your hand when you try to steal my sweet potato fries and sneak handfuls of your popcorn when you're not looking. That beats a party any night."

I had to agree, but then, parties were an unknown quantity as far as I was concerned. I left those to Matt.

NOTE

HINDSIGHT IS a wonderful thing. That brief pang when Matt mentioned going on a date, for example. I told myself at the time that it was nothing, but I think deep down, I was jealous. People gravitated to him so easily, whereas I felt like I continually wore a sign saying Keep Your Distance.

Yeah, I told myself at the time that I was jealous of his popularity. That was it.

Of course, *now*....

What did I say about hindsight?

"OKAY, WHAT did you think?" Matt asked as we exited the movie theater.

"It was... interesting."

He came to a halt in the middle of the sidewalk. "Interesting?"

I stopped too. "What?"

Matt guffawed. "How long have I known you? Long enough to know when you're full of shit. So tell me the truth. It was my choice, but I'm a big boy. I can take it."

I sighed. "All right. I think I would probably have loved it, if…."

"If?"

"If I'd been a little kid. Because let's be honest here, only kids would have been impressed with the CGI."

"Maybe." Then Matt's sigh echoed mine. "You're right, it was totally blah. It was like *Gremlins* meets *The Goonies*, meets… boring as whale shit." He shook his head. "And it was way too long. Time that I'll never get back."

"So my choice next time?"

Matt nodded, then he stilled. "Why do I have the feeling that I may regret saying yes?"

I rubbed my hands together gleefully. "I have one word for you: Disney." Then I ran for my truck as he groaned.

Payback was a bitch.

Chapter Twelve

Spring, 2010

MATT WAS standing in front of the open closets, perusing his wardrobe, his brow furrowed.

"Deciding what to wear to go out to eat?" I leaned against the wall, my arms folded. Friday night was generally when we ate out. It had become a pleasant habit.

Matt inclined his head toward me, still frowning. "Aren't you going to Trey Watmore's party? I thought you got an invite too." Trey was holding a Thank God It's Spring Break party in the house he shared with four other students. Trey's parties had already achieved legendary status on campus. Lots of alcohol, lots of girls, loud music, and a *whole* lotta weed.

Not my thing at all.

I shook my head. "I was going to stay in and wash my hair," I joked. "But you, on the other hand, should definitely go, you being Mr. Popularity and all."

Rather than smile at my humor, Matt scowled. "I'm far from being popular."

I snorted. "Well, you're way more popular than I am, so live with it."

Matt put his hands on his hips, his expression serious. "That does it. You're coming with me."

I went with humor. "Aw, Dad, do I *have* to?"

It sailed right over Matt's head. "I'm serious. You need a party. You need to meet more people, make more friends. And besides… washing your hair?" He rolled his eyes.

"Matt, honestly, you go."

He shook his head. "I don't go to many parties, but I've been to a damn sight more than you have."

Great. He was feeling sorry for me.

"Honestly, it's okay. I'll curl up in a beanbag and read, or maybe watch a DVD. You should go. You'll have a great time."

"Correction: *we'll* have a great time. So get your ass in gear and decide what you're wearing." He speared me with an intense gaze. "And I'm not taking no for an answer."

Crap. He meant it. I knew that don't-mess-with-me-David look.

"Fine." I peered at the hangers, feigning interest, while inside my stomach was churning. I didn't *do* parties. I never had. Parties were for people who knew how to mingle, how to chat about nothing, how to appear witty and fashionable and hip.

Christ, I was none of those things. Now, if you wanted a serious conversation about global warming or the plight of the tiger or even the likelihood of the POTUS achieving a second term in office, I was your man.

Fortunately, one decision was taken out of my hands when Matt took pity on me and pulled out a selection of clothes, thrusting them at me. "Here. Pick something from these."

Jeez, he could be bossy.

THE MUSIC wasn't loud—it was split-your-eardrums *loud*. I hated it with a passion. What was the point of playing music that meant you had to yell above it to carry on a conversation?

The house was packed to the rafters, every available space taken up with bodies. All around me were students engaged in ostensibly fascinating conversations, standing, reclining, leaning, while that music pulsed through everyone and everything, juddering through my bones. Matt was several feet away, talking—make that yelling—to a pretty girl I didn't recognize. I guess she'd come as someone's guest. Matt was smiling and nodding, and every now and then he'd say something and she'd burst into a peal of bright laughter.

It had been like that for the past two hours. I'd stood on the periphery, watching the alcohol consumption and the subsequent flirting of my fellow students, the kissing and the heavier make-out sessions. Most of the time, Matt had stood there with me, before being pulled into a conversation, usually while glancing in my direction, as if he were checking up on me.

Just then the music changed to something a lot quieter and slower paced. Thank God. Out of the corner of my eye, I caught several guys nodding and gesturing toward the rear of the house. I figured it had to be time to roll out the drugs.

"Hey, Matt, want some?" Paul Doyle held up a tightly rolled cigarette. "There's a bunch of us going outside, if you wanna join us."

Matt shook his head. "Thanks, but I'm okay." He went right back to chatting with the girl.

I totally got why Paul had asked him. People like Matt. He has a great sense of humor and the knack of putting people at their ease.

I just seemed to put their backs up.

Then it occurred to me that I hadn't accompanied Matt to many student parties before, and seeing him like that was a revelation. It wasn't as if he was trying hard to fit in with the other guests—he just slipped into the role like it was a well-worn jacket.

The role he always played when it was just the two of us.

"Hey."

I turned my head and came face to face with Greg Tomms, who was in my English class. "Hey." I waited for him to speak. We'd talked in class a couple of times, but then I *always* talked in class. That was just how things were. I answered plenty of questions, proffered explanations, and came up with theories and hypotheses. I was in my element when it came to academic matters. Social niceties were a whole other ball game.

Greg jerked his head toward the kitchen. "The guys just put out more cans of beer if you're interested."

"I'm fine, thanks." I lifted the half-empty plastic cup of God knew what in my hand.

"Oh. Okay." Greg waited a moment longer before giving me a final nod and shuffling off in the direction of a group of three or four students.

I took a sip of the punch, grimacing at its sweetness.

"So, you applied for any jobs yet for after graduation?"

I lowered my cup and turned toward Marsha Selby. I knew her vaguely from around campus. Every time I saw her, there was always a group of guys hovering nearby, each one trying to catch her attention, like birds-of-paradise continually on display. I could understand why. Marsha was pretty, with long blonde hair and pale blue eyes. She came across as sweet, but beyond that, she hadn't been more than a blip on my radar.

"Not yet, no." I'd thought about jobs—we both had—but preparing for finals claimed most of my time.

"Oh." Marsha paused, biting her lip. "So, you think you'll stay in Madison?"

I shrugged. I had no plans to move, but there was always the possibility, once I started looking in earnest for a job.

Marsha held up an empty cup. "I was going to get something to drink. Can I get you something?"

I shook my head. "Thanks, but I'm fine."

Three hours without anyone having a single conversation with me, followed by two stilted attempts to get me talking. I'd had enough.

"Would you excuse me?" I flashed her a polite smile and escaped to the bathroom. Fortunately it was empty, which had to be a first for that evening. I stepped inside, locked the door, and fished my phone out of my jeans pocket. I composed a brief text to Matt.

I'm gonna go. You stay if you want. I wasn't about to spoil his night too.

About a minute later, he replied. *I'll go too. Meet you outside in five?*

Sure.

I washed my hands after I'd poured what was left of the punch down the drain. Outside the bathroom, I deposited the cup in the trash bag provided and slipped through the crowded hall toward the haven of the front door. I grabbed my jacket, once I'd located it under the pile of other coats, and stepped out into the cool night air. I quickly pulled on my jacket and tugged it around me, my mind already contemplating the thirty minutes' walk that was required to get us back to the hall.

Behind me, the door opened and closed. Matt appeared beside me, his thick black jacket pulled tight. Instantly I started walking, the music from the house becoming fainter as I put distance between it and us. Matt said nothing for about five minutes, and I was fine with that. He'd obviously had as poor a time at the party as I had, or else he wouldn't have decided to leave too.

"You wanna tell me what was going on tonight?"

I stiffened at his tone. Matt sounded… annoyed. "What are you talking about?"

Matt let out a barely stifled snort. "You're kidding, right? I've never seen you so… awkward."

I stopped and faced him. "Awkward?"

Matt shrugged. "Uncomfortable. Out of your element. Whatever."

I didn't like the way this conversation was going. "I don't know what you mean." I made as if to continue, but he stopped me with a hand on my arm.

"You had to feel awkward in there, because *I* sure as hell did. You spent most of the night being ignored by everyone, and if that had been me? Yeah, I'd have felt about as welcome as a priest in a house full of devil worshipers." Slowly he withdrew his hand.

I tried to chuckle, but my throat had dried up.

"What I couldn't understand is why." Matt's eyes gleamed in the streetlight. "You're *never* like that with me. You can talk your head off. But just now, back there? You couldn't even say two sentences to Greg."

I froze. "Thanks for the support."

Matt sighed. "I didn't mean to offend you. I'm just trying to get my head around what I saw."

"And what was that?"

Matt paused for a moment. "Two Davids. The one I know like the back of my hand and the one I met tonight." Before I could ask him what he meant, Matt plunged ahead. "I can just about recall what you were like when we first met in second grade, but one thing I *do* remember: you were easier to talk to when you were seven than you were tonight."

"Because it was you," I blurted out.

"Huh?"

I did my best to format the chaotic mess inside my head. "It's always been easy to talk to you, because there's something about you that *makes* it so easy."

Matt stared at me, blinking.

I cleared my throat. "Look, let's just drop it, okay?" There was a heavy lump in my middle, and my tongue was trying to stick to the roof of my mouth. "We're gonna write it off to experience, only to be brought up the next time you invite me to a party." I leveled a hard stare in his direction. "Got it?"

Matt nodded. "Got it." He started walking again, and I kept pace with him, my mind going over his words.

Was I really different with everyone else? And Matt…. He'd never spoken to me like that before. He'd changed so much from the shy boy I'd first met back in second grade.

"By the way," Matt said after a few minutes of silence, as we strolled alongside the lake. "You do realize that Marsha was flirting with you?"

I snorted. "That was flirting? She was asking about job applications. Yeah, *really* sexy."

Matt laughed. "Did you even look at her? The way she was batting her lashes at you?" He shook his head, chuckling. "God, you can be so oblivious sometimes. And what makes this really sad is how she figured that was the way to get you talking. Because, yeah, job applications are *so* not sexy."

I stopped and stared at him. "And who was the one claiming all your attention?"

"Debra. She came with Grant Stephens, but he sort of ditched her to talk sports with his cronies." Matt sighed. "I felt sorry for her, so I struck up a conversation. She seems really sweet." He tugged at my arm. "Come on. We've still got time to catch a movie before bed. I'm in the mood for horror."

"Sounds great." I pushed the party from my mind and focused on a couple of hours of movie and popcorn.

It beat a party any night.

NOTE

READING BACK over what I've written, it occurred to me that the party night revealed a few things.

For one thing, I hadn't realized just how insular mine and Matt's relationship was. When we spent time together, we somehow managed to block out the rest of the world. I liked it like that. But Matt? What surprised me was how he broke out of that insular bubble as often as he did, without even noticing.

Whereas I felt it every single time.

Chapter Thirteen

May, 2010

WHEN MATT'S sigh was forceful enough to stir the pages on which I was writing, I glanced up. "Okay, what's wrong?"

His expression was glum. "I hate job hunting. Especially when I have no clue what to look for."

I put down my pen and leaned back in my chair. "Okay, let's look at this logically. Your strength is math, right?" English was never likely to be his strong suit, even though he'd learned ways to deal with his dyslexia over the years.

"Sure. If you say so."

I chuckled. "Your *professors* say so, numb nuts."

"You leave my nuts outta this." Matt smiled. "Yeah, okay, agreed, I have a head for figures." He speared me with a look. "Whereas you have a head for everything."

I ignored that. "Then let's look at jobs where math would be an asset."

Matt grimaced. "Great. Sounds… riveting."

"We're not looking for a lifelong career here. We're looking for somewhere to get you a toe in the door. A job that might lead on to other jobs, okay?"

Matt shrugged. "I guess." He regarded me keenly. "Is that what you're doing?"

"Absolutely." Granted, I'd had it easier than Matt. The University Book Store had offered me a full-time position, and I'd almost shaken their hand off. I couldn't see me staying there forever, but it was a good first step. Now all we had to do was find an equally good stepping stone for Matt.

He got up from his chair and went over to the little fridge. "Want a soda?"

"Yeah, sounds good."

When Matt sat back down and handed me the cold can, there was a thoughtful expression on his face that I recognized instantly. "Okay, out with it."

Matt blinked. "Jeez. You're good."

"Nope, I just know you, that's all. What's on your mind?"

"Well…." Matt took a long drink of soda. "I kinda assumed we're both looking to stay in Madison, right?"

I nodded.

"So I was thinking that maybe we might get a place together when we graduate." His gaze met mine. "What do you think?"

I laughed. "I *think* we'd be better getting a paycheck sorted first. When we've both got a job to go to, then we can think about where we're gonna live."

"Okay." He didn't sound all that happy, though.

"But in theory? Yeah, I like the idea. Better you living with me than inflicting your bad habits on some unsuspecting roommate." I waggled my eyebrows.

Matt's eyes widened. "*My* bad habits? Look who's talking!"

I laughed. "Less talk, more scouring the job market." Then I dodged the squeezy stress toy that he flung at me.

"SEE YOU next weekend," I called out to Wendy as I walked across the store toward the door.

She smiled from behind the cash desk. "Won't be long until you'll be here full time, right? I heard you got the job. Congratulations."

"Thanks. Yeah, not long now." A couple of weeks and college life would be over. It felt good to have the continuity, however. I glanced at my phone and winced. "Sorry, gotta run. I said I'd meet Matt for a drink." I was keeping my fingers crossed that he'd have good news.

"Say hi to your shadow for me."

I snorted and pushed open the heavy glass door to the bookstore. We'd arranged to meet up at the Crystal Corner bar, and I was running late. Matt had been for an interview with WPS Insurance Corporation for a job in their call center. It wasn't exactly what he wanted, but there was the potential for advancement. WPS was one of the biggest insurance companies in Wisconsin, based right there in Madison.

When I arrived at the bar and grabbed a table, Matt was nowhere in sight. I knew he wouldn't be long—tardy simply didn't exist in his vocabulary—so I ordered a couple of beers.

When a folded newspaper landed in front of me, I gave a start. "Christ, don't do that."

Matt took the seat next to mine, grinning. His gaze alighted on the condensation-covered glass of beer, and he let out a groan. "Yay. I need this." He took a long drink, then smacked his lips when he put down the glass.

"Well?"

Matt did his usual eye roll. "Why don't you at least look at what's in front of you?"

I glanced down at the newspaper, which had been folded to reveal the properties to rent section. For a second or two, it didn't register. Then the ball dropped. "You got the job."

"Sure did." Matt looked absurdly pleased with himself. "So that means…. We can start looking for an apartment."

I held up my beer. "Congratulations."

Matt clinked his glass against mine. "Thanks. And now I'm thinking that I wanna celebrate."

"What did you have in mind?"

His eyes gleamed. "Pizza. And more beer."

I could live with that.

"So, any ideas where we could live?" Matt smiled. "I'm thinking a nice two-bed condo with a view of the lake, parking spots, a pool…."

"Whoa there." I chuckled. "You haven't even looked at rental prices yet, have you?"

Matt sobered pretty quickly. "Ugh, no. Why?"

"We won't be making a whole lotta money for a while. I think the lake view and the pool might have to wait a little longer."

He scowled. "Do you always have to be so damned logical? Can't a guy dream, at least for a little while?"

"Sure. Dream away. Just don't expect me to commiserate when you set your sights on living in a gorgeous apartment, which you then discover we can't afford." I shrugged. "Trying to be practical here."

Matt sighed. "Yeah, you're right." Then he brightened. "Let's forget apartment hunting for now. There are more important issues to be considered."

"Such as?"

He grinned. "What toppings you want on your side of the pizza."

You had to love Matt. Nothing got in the way of a good pizza.

"THIS IS depressing." Matt closed his laptop with a heavy sigh.

I knew what he meant. We'd spent the whole of Sunday morning looking at apartments online, and it was starting to look like a fruitless task. We'd done the math and worked out how much would be coming in, and how much we'd need to pay out in utilities, transportation, food, and anything else we could think of. Then we'd looked at two-bedroom apartments that we could afford.

It was a very, very short list.

"It was a great idea, but it's not gonna work, is it?" I hated to admit defeat, because I really liked the idea of sharing with Matt.

Matt expelled a long breath. "This sucks."

"We could always move back home." Not that I wanted to. I'd had four years of freedom, and much as I loved my parents, I wanted to keep my newfound independence.

"God, no." Matt shuddered. "That would mean sharing a house with Paula. I mean, I love my sister, but God, she's a... *teenager*." Another shudder.

I laughed. I couldn't picture it either.

Matt stilled, his eyes bright. "Wait a second." He opened the laptop and tapped the keyboard, almost buzzing with barely controlled excitement.

"What are you up to?"

"Hush. Let me do this. I'll tell you in a minute or two."

I chuckled. "Jeez, you are so bossy." I got up from my chair. "I'll go fetch the laundry. Want me to collect yours too?"

"Mm-hmm." Matt had his gaze glued to the screen, so I left him to it.

By the time I got back to our room with a basket full of clean clothes, he was sitting there with a huge grin on his face.

"I take it you were successful in whatever you were doing?"

Matt nodded and turned the laptop to face me. "Take a look at this."

I peered at the screen. "Er, Matt? This is a one-bedroom apartment." I lifted my chin to regard him, frowning.

Matt was still grinning. "Correction—it's a *huge* one-bedroom apartment. One thousand square feet of space, to be exact."

"Yes, and it costs $1,300 a month." I looked again. "Matt, this is a luxury condo. What's wrong with it?"

"What do you mean?"

I folded my arms across my chest. "How many apartments have we looked at online? For something this big, we should be looking at a rent of about $1,600 to maybe $1,800. So why is this place so cheap?"

"I don't know!" Matt scraped his hand through his hair. "But have you never heard the phrase, 'Never look a gift horse in the mouth'?"

"There's a reason for that. It'll bite ya. So why are we even looking at this?"

Matt made an impatient noise and grabbed the laptop from me. "You didn't read the small print. The rent includes use of the gym, and—"

"There's a gym?"

Matt nodded gleefully. "And we only need to pay for electricity, because gas and water are included. It has a washer/dryer. There's a rooftop garden, a twenty-four seven grocery store across from it, parking space, and someone on site to take care of the building."

"Yes, but may I point out two things here? One, it still doesn't account for the low price, and two, it *still* only has one bedroom," I stressed patiently.

Matt rolled his eyes. "Duh. I know that. But the room looks big enough to accommodate two beds. Two *big* beds." That grin was back. "Come on. We've shared a room for three years. It's not like we're not used to each other by now, right?"

He had a point.

"Can we at least go look at it?" Matt's eyes were wide and full of hope.

Like I wanted to rain on his parade. "Sure, we can look."

Matt did a fist pump. "Yes!" He reached for his phone.

"What are you doing?" I couldn't keep the amusement out of my voice.

"Calling to make an appointment to view it."

I had to laugh. "Matt? It's Sunday. They're closed."

His pout made me laugh even harder.

NOTE

OF COURSE, once we got to see the apartment, we soon learned why the price was lower. Its location wasn't ideal—it was next to the gym—but we could live with that. Then we found out that the previous tenant had up and left, and the landlord was trying to rent it quick. It was in need of some TLC. The paint was peeling in places, and the previous tenants hadn't been all that careful with the property.

The landlord took one look at our application form, saw we both had jobs, and that was that. I think we were definitely a step up from his last tenants. Then Matt had the bright idea of offering to repaint the whole apartment if the landlord bought all the materials.

Yeah, that went down really well, with the landlord at least.

I figured Matt might be in for a surprise when he saw me in action with a paintbrush.

DAD LEFT us in the living room and headed for the bathroom, checking the details on the sheet we'd given him.

Matt leaned closer. "What's he doing?" he whispered.

"He said if we were serious about renting this place, he wanted to check it out first."

Matt smiled. "That's kinda sweet." He gestured toward the bedroom. "So what's your mom doing?"

I chuckled. "Would you believe, measuring for drapes?" We hadn't even signed the rental agreement yet. Dad had insisted on viewing the apartment before we put a pen to paper.

Matt laughed. "I love your parents."

Dad came back into the living room. "The plumbing looks sound. It's a good size, guys." He glanced around. "There's even space for a dining table." Dad grinned. "So be prepared for your mom deciding to come for lunch." He gazed at the walls. "Yeah, it sorely needs a paint job. You two will have your work cut out for you. What's the plan—paint first, then move your stuff in? That might be the easiest solution."

Matt nodded. "We thought the same thing. The landlord said once we've signed, we can get to work on it. We should have it ready for after graduation."

Mom came into the room. "In spite of the state of the place, this is great. Are you boys sure you can afford this?"

Before either of us could reply, Dad responded. "Sarah, I'm sure they wouldn't be contemplating renting it if they hadn't worked out their finances." He peered at us. "Right?"

I smiled confidently. "Right." Matt had been correct. We could afford it. Just.

"I think it's great that you two are sharing," Mom said with a smile. "And there's plenty of room for all your stuff that's still in the attic," she added. "Not to mention Speedy and Turbo. I think it's high time those turtles lived with you." Mom and Dad had taken care of my little guys while I'd lived in the hall.

Matt snorted. "That's it. She's finally getting you out of the house. Next thing you know, your bedroom will be her craft room."

Mom flushed guiltily. "I was just thinking that it would be good for you to have all your things around you, that's all."

I hugged her tightly. "It's all right, Mom. Don't you listen to Matt's teasing. You can do whatever you like with my room, once I've moved out." I released her.

To my surprise her eyes glistened, and she quickly wiped them with her hand.

Dad walked over and put his arm around her shoulders. "Hey, none of that. He has to leave sometime, right?" He dug into his pants pocket and pulled out a folded handkerchief. "Here."

Mom took it, sniffing. "I'm sorry. It just hit me that my baby is all grown up."

I glanced over to where Matt was watching us, smiling. I shook my head. "Wait until it's your mom, dude." It felt kinda unreal.

A week until college was finally over. Both of us with jobs. A rented apartment—well, it would be ours once we signed the paperwork.

I guess it was the start of Real Life.

Man, that was a scary thought.

"IS THAT all of it?" I asked my dad when he came back into the living room, his arms full.

Dad nodded. "That's the last of it." He glanced at the piles of boxes stacked up around us. "It's gonna take you a while to get all this sorted." He gave me a wry smile. "You can manage it all this weekend, right?"

I laughed. I started work on Monday. "Yeah, sure." We'd probably have to put up with the boxes for a little longer than that.

Dad gazed around him. "You guys did a neat job of the painting. If I'd known you were that proficient at it, I'd have had you painting the house years ago."

I wasn't about to mention the fact that Matt was definitely more adept when it came to wielding a paintbrush. He'd taken one look at my efforts to paint alongside a doorframe and solemnly handed me the roller.

It was like being a little kid again. I could never stay inside the lines.

Matt came out of the bedroom, his dad behind him. "Okay, we've assembled the beds."

Dad chuckled. "Is there space to get around them?"

Matt's dad laughed. "Not until they empty more boxes. At least there's a large closet."

I ran my fingers through my hair. "Y'know, it didn't look like we had this much stuff when everything was in the U-Haul."

Matt snorted. "That's because I am a master at tessellating. If there was a space, I filled it. This is why *I* packed the van while *you* did the heavy work."

"I did wonder about that." I narrowed my gaze. "*One* of us got off easy."

Both our dads laughed. "And you still think it's a good idea, these two living together?" Matt's dad asked mine.

"As long as they sort out their own squabbles, I'm okay with it," my dad said with a shrug.

"Hey, we *are* right here, y'know." I glared at them.

"Yes, and if you can find your shower stuff amid all this chaos and get cleaned up, we're taking you both to dinner." Dad grinned at my open mouth. "What, you didn't think we were going to celebrate getting rid of—I mean, you both leaving home?" He winked. "We've reserved a table at Naples 15. You two, Matt's parents and Paula, and your mom and I."

I had the best parents.

Correction: *we* had the best parents.

NOTE

THE REALLY strange thing about moving into an apartment with Matt was that it felt… normal. I supposed at the time that it was because we'd already shared a room for so long, we felt comfortable around each other. Certainly the move from the hall to the condo was almost seamless, and it wasn't long before we settled into our routines. Matt started his new job, and it became clear that promotion would be sooner rather than later. He was happy with that, and I was glad that he was finally in a place where he felt at ease.

Chapter Fourteen

NAPLES 15 was packed, as usual, and our table was rowdy like it always was when we got together. Matt was squeezed in between me and his mom, my parents and Paula facing us, and his dad at the end. It was a tight fit.

It was kinda bittersweet. I loved it when our families spent time together, and I knew logically that there would be plenty of occasions in the future for more such gatherings—like Mom would go without cooking Christmas dinner for all of us; it had become a holiday tradition—but this night was different. Matt and I were about to embark on a new adventure. We were venturing out into the big, cruel world where if something went wrong, we couldn't go back to our parents and hope they'd make everything all right. It was time for us to deal with our own issues.

It was exciting. It was also scary as hell.

What made the evening interesting was that it felt like there was an undercurrent, something bubbling below the surface. Maybe it was the looks I intercepted between our parents. Nothing too overt, but yeah, definitely something brewing. So when my dad stood up at the end of the meal, when the coffee had arrived and Matt was trying to steal Paula's mint from her saucer, the skin on the back of my neck prickled.

Dad pinned me and Matt with a hard stare. "Okay, so… I know this is an exciting time for you both—"

"And you're not going to need us anymore," Mom added with a sniff.

Maryann patted her hand. "It's okay. I'll come over and bring wine and chocolate." That raised a few laughs.

"For God's sake, it's not like we're moving to Alaska," I remonstrated. "We're gonna be about fifteen minutes by car."

Dad cleared his throat. "If I may be allowed to continue?" Everyone did their best to quiet down, but there were still snickers. "Anyway, we—that's your mom and I, plus Daniel and Maryann—talked about it and we came to the conclusion that you two are basically homebodies. Other than Matt moving away and then coming back, the two of you haven't really been anywhere. So we got to thinking that maybe what you needed was a chance to go out and see something you may never have the opportunity to experience." His gaze alighted on me. "Real life takes over, and things you always wanted to do have a habit of getting farther and farther away."

I think that was the first moment I saw my dad, *really* saw him, past the persona I'd always known, to the man underneath. Because in that bubble of time, we were two men, not just father and son. I have to say, it sent a shiver through me.

I guess we're all grown up.

Then I pushed the thought aside. *Not just yet.*

My dad glanced across at my mom, and she reached into her purse, withdrawing a long envelope that she handed to Matt and I with a flourish.

"What's this?"

Mom rolled her eyes. "Well, if you open it, maybe you'll find out."

I tore the seal and reached inside to find….

No. No fucking way.

Matt stared at the airline tickets, and his eyes widened when he saw the destination. "Costa Rica?"

I couldn't believe it. "I don't understand." I really didn't. When could we go to Costa Rica? We had jobs and an apartment and…. But damn, my heart was pounding at the thought.

"We want you to have an adventure before you settle down to real life. Go out and see something that the two of you have always wanted to see." He gazed at Matt. "Something that until now you've only glimpsed on TV or in the pages of the National Geographic."

Beside me, I caught the hitch in Matt's breathing.

"Think of all the things you can do there," Daniel added. "Trek the rainforests. Bungee jump—"

"Oh, hell no. Uh-uh. No bungee jumping." Maryann glared at him.

Daniel laughed. "Sorry, honey, but you have to let go of the cord sometime." He winked at us. "On second thoughts? No letting go of the cord if you're bungee jumping." That gave us a good laugh. "The point is, do something wild and reckless. Live a little, then come home and worry about where the rest of your lives will take you."

Matt sighed. "I hate to be the practical one here—"

I guffawed. "Hey, I thought that was my job."

He whacked me on the arm. "I'm being serious here. We have jobs, remember? Mine starts Monday."

His dad coughed. "Ugh, no, it doesn't."

Matt blinked. "Excuse me?"

"I met with your boss last week. I told him what we were planning, and he said that he was willing to have you start two weeks later." He glanced at me. "Same thing for you. They've known at the bookstore this past week."

Okay, that was when my jaw dropped.

Matt wasn't done yet. "This has to have cost you a fortune." I knew he was thinking about his parents.

His mom leaned across and kissed his cheek. "We'd always intended giving you a graduation present. *I* wanted to give you a car, but *no*, your *daddy* wants to give you the opportunity to break your neck, zip-lining, or canyoning, or white-water rafting, or whatever else you're gonna put your mind to while you're there." She gave Daniel a mock glare before continuing. "I admit, this sounds more fun than a car, just as long as you're both careful."

"I'll take care of him. I promise," I intoned solemnly. Like I'd let Matt get hurt.

Matt shook his head, chuckling. "Face it, they've covered everything."

And that was when I let myself start to get excited. It was weird. I'd never given much thought, if any, to visiting Costa Rica, but the idea of going there with Matt was exhilarating. Hell, going *anywhere* with Matt would be fun. I grinned at him. "It beats camping, I suppose."

"Dude. Camping in Lake Mendota Park—versus Costa Freaking *Rica*? Are you out of your mind? It's gonna be epic!" He was almost dancing on his chair. "Thanks, guys. This is awesome!"

"We're not being all that original," my dad remarked.

"What do you mean?"

"Well, when I asked your mother to marry me, your grandparents did the same for us. There was no way we could even think about going on a trip, and I suppose they didn't want us to be forever feeling that we'd never done anything."

I couldn't believe I was hearing this for the first time. "Where did you go?"

Mom gave us a shy smile. "He took me to Paris, and it was everything I'd imagined. Beautiful, romantic, and if such a thing were possible, it made the two of us fall even more deeply in love." Then she laughed. "Not quite the same thing as trekking through a rainforest, visiting a volcano, going to—"

"There's a volcano?" It was my turn to shift impatiently on my seat. "When do we leave?"

Matt dug me in the ribs with his elbow. "How about we finish our coffee first?"

Yeah. Two weeks with Matt, on what was beginning to sound like the trip of a lifetime.

I couldn't wait.

"We've booked you a self-drive holiday." This was from my dad. "That way, you get to see as much of Costa Rica as you want."

Before I could reply, Matt fixed me with a stern look. "I'm driving."

"Hey!" I knew I sounded indignant, but right then I didn't give a shit. "I am more than capable of—"

Matt folded his arms. "I'm driving. Non-negotiable."

When our dads started laughing, I knew it was a lost cause.

At least this way, we stood a chance of getting home in one piece.

MATT STARED at me, his mouth open. "Are you kidding me?"

That made me feel a whole lot better. "Just because *you* don't question the Good Lord's wisdom in not giving us wings, doesn't mean the rest of us have to go along with you." I was gripping the armrests so tightly, my fingers were white. Heaven knew what I'd be like when the plane actually started moving.

"Why didn't you tell me you were nervous about flying?"

I gave him a look that was pure *duh*. "Because up until the moment I sat in this seat and realized that this hefty great metal thing was actually going up into the sky, I didn't know, *never having flown before*." It had come as a complete surprise to me too. The nearer we got to the plane, the faster my heart started racing.

Yes, I knew it was illogical. Yes, I knew people flew every damn day, all over the world. I was just having a hard time imagining *me* doing it. For one thing? That plane looked awfully heavy….

Then a member of the cabin crew passed by and leaned over. "Are you okay?"

I swear, it was on the tip of my tongue to fling back at him "Do I *look* okay to you?"

"He's fine," Matt interjected quickly. "First time flyer, that's all." He patted my hand.

"Well, we're here to help in any way we can. If you'd like me to talk you through what actually happens during a flight, maybe even ask the pilot to show you the cockpit, I—"

"I'm sure I'll be just fine," I said, lying through my teeth. He didn't seem convinced, so I pasted on a bright smile. "Honestly, if I need help, I'll ask for it."

He gave a nod, smiled at Matt, then carried on his way down the aisle.

Before I could say a word, Matt got there first. "I got an idea." He bent down and pulled his backpack from where he'd stuffed it under the seat in front. From inside, he removed some sheets of paper stapled together. "Here. I printed these off before we left. It's the details your dad emailed us about the trip." He thrust them into my hands. "We have some reading to do."

"Huh?"

"Well, with everything happening so fast, we haven't had time to look at all the cool stuff they've picked for us to do."

Fast? I'd been amazed that getting a passport had only taken forty-eight hours. He was right, of course. And reading would certainly take my mind off my present circumstances.

Matt pointed to various sections in the notes. "It says we get to do zip-lining near the volcano. And there are a couple of places where you can find…." He paused, his eyes sparkling. "Turtles."

"Really?" God, I felt like I was a teenager all over again.

Matt nodded. "White-water rafting, snorkeling, watching whales and dolphins…. Man, this place has it all."

I took the sheets and started reading. It was only when I felt a rumbling through me that I looked up. "What was that?"

"Oh, just the plane taking off." Matt uttered the words like it was an everyday occurrence.

"Whoa, we took off?" I tried to peer through the window, but he stopped me, tapping the sheets with his finger.

"Trust me, you're much better off looking at that than what's going on out there."

I glared at him. "Did you do that on purpose?"

"What?" Yeah, Matt couldn't do innocent to save his life.

"Distract me."

He blinked, then grinned. "Maybe? Did it work?" He patted my hand again. "Think of it this way. If you can go up in a plane, canyoning is going to be child's play."

"Remind me again. What's canyoning?"

Matt's grin widened. "Rappelling down a waterfall. Actually, several waterfalls."

Okay, that sounded like it might be a lot of fun. And now that the plane had leveled off, things felt a little more... stable.

As long as I didn't try to think all that hard about where we were.

"I THOUGHT we'd pick up the four-by-four at the airport," Matt said quietly from the other queen bed.

I chuckled. "You know those notes you were so keen for me to read on the plane? If you'd actually read them, you'd have recalled that we get it tomorrow. One night here in San José, then tomorrow they take us to the Arenal Springs hotel. *Then* we get the vehicle, Mr. Impatient."

"How can you be so cool about this? I mean, we're gonna be staying near a freaking *volcano*!"

Okay, sleep obviously wasn't in the cards. I switched on the lamp and sat up, leaning against the pillows. "I'm trying to pace myself. I don't want to run out of excitement on the first night," I teased. Matt threw a pillow at me, which I deftly deflected. "And if you're going to be doing all the driving, then maybe it would be a good idea to get some sleep." I wasn't about to let him know I was just as excited as he was.

I'd never imagined going on such a trip, and it still felt unreal, like any minute I was going to wake up and it would all have been a dream.

"Hey, if I'm in charge of the driving, what are you in charge of?"

"You. And the camera," I added as an afterthought.

Matt snorted. "God help us, then. We'll be going home with a lot of photos with missing heads and blurred landscapes. I've seen your efforts at photography, remember?"

"I promise I will do my best to make every goddamn photo a masterpiece, okay?" I wasn't about to contradict him. There was a reason my mom always gave the camera to my dad whenever photos were required.

I switched off the light. "And now, go to sleep, or you'll look all bleary-eyed in the amazing photos I'm gonna take tomorrow."

If Matt's snort was anything to go by, he didn't believe me.

Chapter Fifteen

THE ARENAL Volcano was the majestic backdrop to our first zip-lining experience, and below us was the jungle, deep and dense and green. Not exactly quiet, however.

"What are we hearing?" I asked one of our guides, Wesley.

He grinned. "Howler monkeys." Then he pointed to the platform where Matt was donning his safety helmet. "You guys ready?"

Judging by the way Matt was almost bouncing on the spot, I figured we were. Wesley and I walked up the path to the platform. Matt was beaming at me.

"Isn't this awesome?" The three tourists who stood near him were grinning too.

His enthusiasm was infectious, and excitement bubbled up inside me. "Yeah, it is."

"So, do you guys want to go across singly or together?"

Matt jerked his head toward me, and I nodded eagerly. "Together," we shouted in unison. I'd had no idea such a thing was possible.

Wesley laughed. "Yeah, I thought you'd like that idea." He got me to stand behind Matt, and then he connected our harnesses together at the waist. "Okay, guys, one hand on the line the whole way across, if you want to. You can hold on to the harness line with the other. Or you can pretend you're flying. You wouldn't be the first tourists to do that."

Once we were hooked up, it was time for that push to send us sailing out above the canopy of trees. And Oh My God, yes, it felt like we were flying. Matt squealed loudly the entire way, and joy filled me to be sharing this with him. It was effortless, speeding through the air, and such a rush. When we came to the end, I wanted to do it all over again. Matt was laughing, pointing up to where we'd just come from, and I knew he had the same idea.

"Don't worry. There are enough stations for you to do this all day if you want to," the guide told us. "That's the great thing about Costa Rica. There's so much to do, that you'll be spoiled for choice."

"Then let's do it again!"

I don't think I'd ever seen Matt so happy, and I decided then and there on my mission for our time in Costa Rica: I was going to make him smile every single day.

MATT EYED the mud bath with trepidation. "It looks… icky."

I laughed. "Okay, granted, but they said the way your skin feels when it comes off is wonderful."

Matt didn't look convinced. "So what do we do—sit in it?" He regarded the pool of mud, his nose wrinkled.

I hadn't told him the best part. "Not exactly." Trying my hardest not to giggle, I scooped up a handful of warm gray-green mud and flung it straight at his swim trunks.

His eyes widened, and he squeaked, "Hey, what was that for?"

The girl on duty at the mud bath rolled her eyes. "There's always one." She gave me a stern look, but I could tell she was trying not to laugh. "You're supposed to smear the mud all over you, then let it dry off."

Matt's eyes gleamed. "Can I smear him?" He pointed toward me.

She laughed. "Go for it. I won't tell a soul." Before I could get a word in, he filled both hands with mud and launched himself at me, then covered my chest and smeared it over my shoulders.

Like I was gonna stand for that.

With a lot of giggling, the two of us got the mud pretty much everywhere. Well, nearly everywhere.

"Close your eyes!" I yelled, a split second before I rubbed muddy hands over his face.

"Mmmph!" I stepped back, and Matt opened his scrunched-ups eyes, the only pale spots in a now gray-green face. Then he grinned. "Now it's my turn."

"Hell no." I tried to run away from him, but instead I tumbled face-first into the mud. When I got up, spluttering and wiping mud from my eyes and lips, Matt was almost doubled over, laughing his ass off.

It didn't take long before the mud had dried to a stiff crust, and we were pointed toward the hot springs. Steam rose from the surface of the bubbling water, and there was even a bar nearby. We stepped into the hot water and sank down into it, leaning back against the rocks that surrounded the springs.

Talk about heaven….

"This feels amazing," Matt said with a sigh, his eyes closed as he wiped a wet hand over his face to remove the mud crust. "I could sit in this all day."

I chuckled. "Do that and there'll be Boiled Matt on the menu for tonight." It did feel pretty wonderful, I had to admit. We sat on the ledge below the water's surface and let the warmth soak into our bones. With all the mud finally gone, I got the bartender to pour us a couple of cocktails, and we lounged in the water, sipping the orange and yellow concoctions.

"Okay, change of adjective." Matt smiled. "This feels decadent."

"Of course, you know what's gonna feel even better?"

He opened one eye. "What?"

"A dip in the pool."

I swear, that smile of his could power a small town. "*Now* you're talking!"

Madison—and work—seemed a damn sight farther away than a seven-hour flight.

I SLID open the patio door and gazed out at the Pacific Ocean. "This is incredible." The sky was black, dusted with stars, and the silver moon was reflected on the surface of the ocean.

Matt walked up behind me. "Isn't it? I've loved the activities, but there's something to be said for having a room that looks out onto the ocean. Soft white sand, a warm breeze. This really is paradise." He nudged me. "Did you see the jacuzzi? And there's an outside shower too."

I snickered. "Yeah. Pity there's only one bed."

Matt snorted. "Now, if you snored, that would be an issue. Thankfully, I know you don't, so we're all good."

I chuckled. "Never mind that. If you hog all the covers, *someone* will find himself sleeping out on the deck tonight." I smiled sweetly. "At least you won't be on your own."

"Why? Who'll be out there with me?"

"Not who—more of a what. We're talking howler monkeys, squirrels, iguanas, porcupines, geckos, armadillos, frogs, raccoons—oh, and not forgetting skunks."

Matt's eyes were huge. "There's that much wildlife out there?" When I nodded, he grabbed his phone. "Well, what are we waiting for? Let's go hunting. The one who photographs the least amount of wildlife gets to do all the packing."

I always loved a challenge.

"I'M NOT sure about this," Matt murmured, staring down into the waterfall pool some thirty feet below us.

"We managed the last jump," I argued. "And that was great, wasn't it?"

"Yeah, but that was only twelve feet. This is more than double."

I leaned closer. "Think of it as something to tell the grandkids when they ask what grandpa got up to when he was younger."

He snorted. "Excuse me? What makes you think I want kids, let alone grandkids?"

"Okay," I amended. "Think of it as something to tell Darren's kids, to prove what a cool uncle you are."

Matt nodded, standing up straight. "Now *that* I can get behind. There's one thing we haven't tried yet, though."

"What's that?"

"Tandem jump!" he yelled, grabbing my hand as he leaped off the platform.

Christ, I thought my heart was about to burst as we hurtled down toward the pool. The sudden rush of cold water around me was exhilarating, and as I burst through the surface into the light, Matt was doing the same, laughing and spluttering.

"You dick!" I shouted, amid laughter.

"Admit it. You loved every second of it!" Matt flung back at me, bobbing up and down in the water.

I couldn't deny it, but I was already thinking of ways to exact my revenge.

IT WAS the perfect way to end the vacation.

We lay on soft sand, the beach bar only a few feet away from our loungers. The temperature was perfect, and the sun was beginning its descent.

I didn't want it to end, however. It had been twelve days of heaven, as far as I was concerned, and the thought of the flight home the following day left me filled with an ache. It was more than just the vacation, I knew that. It had been wonderful to spend time with Matt, filling our days with laughter and the sheer joy of being alive.

"So, ready to do all our packing tonight?" Matt murmured.

"Ugh, excuse me? I photographed the most animals, remember?"

Matt let out an explosive snort. "Dude. The deal was not to photograph the largest amount of *one species*, so your collection of howler monkeys doesn't count, however impressive it may be. I, on the other hand, caught a raccoon, a squirrel, two armadillos, a porcupine, a—"

"That's right, rub it in." I still couldn't believe he'd managed to get so many.

"It's okay." Matt's voice softened. "You just pack your own suitcase. I already did mine this morning while you were showering."

"You did? God, you're sneaky."

Matt gave me a superior smile. "I prefer to think of it as being stealthy. Maybe I should consider another career. Ninja, maybe."

I burst out laughing. "Think again. That *was* you before, wasn't it? Yelling because you stepped on something spiky when you were coming along the path to our room?"

Matt gave me a mock glare. "Do you have to hear everything?" He sat up and grabbed his towel. "I'm gonna have a shower before dinner."

As he got up from the lounger, I caught hold of his arm. "We okay?"

He gave me a warm smile. "Always. And in case I forget to tell you, I've had a wonderful vacation." He winked. "I've got the photos to prove it."

"Hang on, I'll come with you."

Matt grinned. "Race you. Last one there gets the outside shower!" And he was off, dashing over the sand toward the path that led to our room, me in hot pursuit.

NOTE

I WOULDN'T change one minute of that vacation. It had been a delightful surprise and then gone on to be a wonderful collection of memories that I will treasure for the rest of my life.

Sharing it with Matt made it just... perfect.

Chapter Sixteen

October, 2013

AFTER THREE years of sharing an apartment, we were a well-oiled machine.

Okay, so I'd progressed from Slob-in-Training to Full-Blown Slob, and Matt had quickly adjusted to his new role as Cleaner-Upper of David's Mess, but hey, it worked. One benefit to having a kitchen rather than the microwave oven in our room was that I discovered how much I loved to cook, and I was pretty good at it. Matt, on the other hand, hated cooking, so it all worked out pretty well. He took care of our apartment, and I ensured that we were both well fed. We shopped together for groceries, and the store across the street got to know us really well, especially when Matt got the munchies and raided their shelves for snacks and pizza.

Not that there wasn't the occasional grinding of gears in our machine when arguments occurred, but they tended to be for the silliest reasons. Like when we shopped for produce and I insisted on squeezing the mangoes and the avocados before I placed them in the cart. Well, I mean… you have to make sure they're ripe, right? But every time I did it, Matt would huff and tell me not to do that.

NOTE

SOMETIMES I did it just to piss him off. I loved it when he got riled. And it got so that the shopping assistants would laugh at us arguing. Not in a mean way—they said we were like some old married couple and that it was kinda cute.

That usually cracked us up, and the arguments would pretty much die right there. Not that I'd ever had a really serious argument with Matt. We didn't gripe about what channel to watch, whose turn it was to take out the trash—that's because it was always Matt's turn—or do the laundry. Life was just... smooth.

WELL, VIRTUALLY smooth.

You know how when you know someone really well, you finish their sentences for them, know what they're gonna say next, even find you're doing the same things they are? Well, Matt and I took that to a whole new level.

We both got girlfriends at the same time.

I met Maxine in the bookstore when she came to buy a birthday present for her dad, who was a total Badger fan. I spent maybe twenty minutes taking her around, making suggestions, and finally she made a decision. What I didn't expect was her turning up the following day to thank me for being so helpful. That was kinda sweet.

When she kept popping back to the store over the next couple of weeks, I sorta got the impression that she wasn't there to buy a book or more Badger apparel. And when she asked one day if I'd like to go for a coffee or a drink or something when I finished work, I said yes.

As dates go—and yeah, that's exactly what it was—it was a pleasant first experience. Matt got in a lot of digs about it being time I dipped my toes into the waters, but I paid him no mind. Then when he said he'd invited a girl from his office out for dinner and asked if we wanted to double date, I agreed.

It was a great night, and I really had a good time. Maxine and Matt's date, Rachel, got along very well, and in spite of my nerves, I was able to relax. By the end of the night, I was truly wondering why I'd waited so long to ask someone out, because it had been enjoyable.

Maxine and I dated a couple of times more, and then things took an inevitable turn.

I'd known it was coming, of course, and I have to admit, I was nervous. I was twenty-two and a virgin, with a more experienced girlfriend. Not that I was a complete novice, you understand—porn has its uses, apart from the obvious—but yeah, I approached that first time with no small amount of trepidation. My only goal was that she enjoyed it. That wasn't me being altruistic—that was me hoping that my lack of experience wasn't totally obvious.

Let's just say the evening was not a rousing success and leave it there, all right?

We went out on a couple more dates and attempted another night in Maxine's bed. And no, not gonna talk about *that* night either. By this point I was starting to think that I wasn't cut out for sexual adventures. What made it worse was that Maxine clearly had the same idea. We called it a day after that.

Don't get me wrong, she was great. She was patient with my... not so skilled efforts, and she *seemed* enthusiastic. And it *was* good. Better than. But there was something missing too. I enjoyed her company, but she didn't make me feel... I'm not even sure what I thought she should make me feel. I just knew it wasn't there. Nor was it there the other times I went out with people I met at the bookstore, or at the coffee shop, or....

Let me say this: these experiences helped me. I became a little less shy and a little more outgoing. Okay, not all *that* much more outgoing, but it was still a start.

The funny thing was, Matt and Rachel didn't last all that long either. A fine pair, we were.

NOTE

WANT TO know the really weird part?

Neither Matt nor I ever talked about our dates. I mean, they just didn't come up in conversation. Not a single word.

Looking back, I think we were both looking for something from a relationship, and we didn't find it. Maybe because we were looking in the wrong place the whole time, only we never realized.

THERE WAS one routine that never changed, and that was the family Sunday lunch. Mom insisted that I attend, seeing as the apartment wasn't that far from the house, and I didn't really mind. It made her happy, and that was always a plus. Besides, Matt always came with me, and sometimes his parents and sister would join us.

I liked that our families got along. It would have been awkward if that wasn't the case, but I guess they'd gotten to know one another really well after all the years that Matt and I had been friends. I was constantly told that it wasn't "sir" and "ma'am" but "Daniel" and "Maryann." Jeez, that was hard. I mean, I'd known them for most of my life, and my parents had drummed into me from an early age the importance of respect. And they were no different, insisting that Matt call them by their first names. Of course, sometimes we forgot, because it really took some getting used to.

We were at my parents' house for lunch one Sunday when the topic of Darren's kids came up. Darren and Gail had a little girl, Lindy, who was four, and baby Jesse, who was eighteen months. Mom was always asking after them—if Matt had seen them lately, if he had any recent pictures. I found those conversations amusing. Matt liked his nephew and niece, sure, but in small doses, and I was in complete agreement on that one.

It was a funny thing, but I couldn't see myself as a dad. When that thought had first occurred to me, I'd felt guilty, because isn't that what everyone did? Have kids, I mean? Not that I'd ever admitted to my parents that the probability was pretty high that they wouldn't be grandparents, not unless I really changed as I got older. But hey, I was already twenty-four and awfully set in my ways.

Then it happened. The dreaded question.

Mom smiled at Matt. "Do you want children one day?"

What happened next was sort of funny. Matt said vehemently, "God, no," and I snorted at exactly the same moment. Then we looked at each other and laughed. It wasn't something we'd ever discussed, but it appeared like we were on the same page. As usual.

Mom gazed across at Maryann and sighed. "Oh well." Maryann nodded, like she wasn't surprised by the revelation. Matt regarded me in amusement and gave a casual shrug.

Kids just weren't on our radar.

Christmas, 2013

"DAVID, THERE'S still some turkey left, if you want it."

I moaned. "Do I have Garbage Disposal Unit tattooed on my forehead or something? Because I swear you're just offering me everything that's left on the table." Mom had outdone herself that year, and the dining room table had groaned under the weight of her Christmas Day dinner.

Next to me, Matt laughed. "She's only offering because she knows damn well you'll eat it. David, the Human Vacuum." Around the table, his parents chuckled, and Paula gave me that kind of superior look that only an eighteen-year-old girl knows how to really nail.

I made an attempt to whack Matt on the arm but curtailed it when something rolled in my belly. "Oh God." I shoved back my chair and darted toward the bathroom, praying I'd make it.

Only just. I fell to my knees and brought back my dinner, my stomach heaving, sweat popping out on my brow. Great. Just what I needed—coming down with something during the holidays.

There was a quiet knock on the door. "Hey, you all right?" Matt's voice was soft.

"One second." I wiped my mouth and flushed the toilet before rising to my feet to rinse my mouth out. Then I opened the door and he stepped inside. "Not really," I said weakly, the muscles in my stomach aching. "Maybe I overdid it with dinner." I was half joking, because something in my mind was putting two and two together, and I didn't like the answer.

Judging by Matt's expression, he'd done the math too. "Uh-uh. Not buying it. You've been feeling off for a couple of days now. Didn't you complain about a bellyache over the weekend?"

I nodded.

Matt's gaze was focused on my face. "And it's now Wednesday and you still feel rough. Anything else troubling you?" When I hesitated, he rolled his eyes heavenward. "Great. Out with it."

"I had a little bout of diarrhea, that's all." I kept my tone light, but I knew as soon as I said it that he'd switch into Mother Hen mode. Sometimes he was *so* like my mom, it was scary.

"Do we need to get you to a doctor?" His eyes were filled with concern.

I snorted. "Dude, be serious. It's the holidays. The only place you could take me would be the emergency room, and I'm nowhere near bad enough for that. Besides, that would frighten my mom to death."

Matt surprised me by placing his hand gently on my forehead. "You have a slight fever, you know. And your face is flushed." The lightness of his touch was pleasant.

When he withdrew his hand, I straightened. "Okay, this is what's going to happen. You and I are going back in there, and as far as my parents and anyone else is concerned, I ate too much, all right? I'll put up with the comments and the jokes until it's time to go home. Then I'll have an early night and be right as rain by the morning. You'll see." I spoke with far more confidence than I felt.

"If you say so." Matt still didn't appear convinced. There was a reason for that, of course. He knew me far too well.

I HAD no idea what woke me. Then I felt coolness against my forehead. "Whaaa?" I was kinda groggy.

"Shhh." Matt's voice came from right beside me. "It's late. You woke me up. You were whimpering and moaning."

"I was?" I had a vague recollection of some dark, twisted dream where I'd been trying to escape... something, but I hadn't been able to shake it. "Sorry." My gut clenched, and I sat upright, shivering. "Oh God, I need the bathroom." Matt got out of my way, and I ran, just making it in time to throw up again. Only now I was aware of how chilled I felt.

Matt was suddenly at my side, handing me toilet paper while he slowly rubbed my back. I wiped my mouth and struggled to stand.

"Here. I'm helping you get back to your bed." His arm was around my shoulder, and I leaned against him, my legs shaking.

I felt like shit.

When he'd gotten me into bed, Matt perched on the edge of the mattress, regarding me with those serious blue eyes. "Does it hurt anywhere?"

I nodded. "My belly."

Matt gazed at me for a moment. "Okay, I'm just gonna try something." He stretched out his hand and placed it gently over my navel, on top of the sheet. "Here?" He exerted the tiniest amount of pressure.

I stifled a moan. "A little." Then he moved his hand lower and to the right, and I just about hit the ceiling. "Christ!"

Matt pulled back instantly. "Okay, that does it. I'm getting you dressed, and then I'm taking you to the emergency room."

"Seriously?"

Matt glared at me and brought his hand to hover over the area where he'd just pressed. "Want me to do that again?"

"Hell no." Just the thought made me break out in a sweat. Then I realized that was the fever.

Matt nodded. "Sit up, and I'll get you some clothes."

Carefully, *so* carefully, he helped me dress and then guided me out of the apartment toward my car. Once he had me buckled up in the passenger seat, Matt got in.

"Where are you taking me?"

"The ER at University Hospital. I'll drive slowly, okay?"

I closed my eyes, aware of the chills that spread throughout my body and the feelings of nausea. God, what was wrong with me?

It wasn't long before Matt had helped me through the main door and was calling a nurse.

Everything got blurry after that while they poked and prodded me, asking questions, but not so much that I didn't catch the doctor's diagnosis.

Apparently I had appendicitis and they were going to operate.

As the orderly wheeled me to a ward, Matt called out after us. "I'm gonna call your parents. Then I'll come find you."

I raised my hand, then dropped it onto the pale blue sheet that covered me.

Surgery. Wow.

I sort of dozed in and out for a while, and then I grew aware of a presence at my bedside, a hand clasped around mine. "Hey. Your folks are on their way."

I turned my head slightly on the pillow to look at Matt. "Did you know?"

"Huh?"

"When you pressed that point and I just about leaped up off the bed… did you know it might be appendicitis?"

"It was a possibility."

I stared at him. "But… how? How did you know?"

"Doesn't everyone know the symptoms of appendicitis?"

"Well, *I* didn't."

Matt smiled. "That just goes to show David Lennon doesn't know everything." He squeezed my hand. "They're not going to wait to operate, the nurse said."

"It's that bad?" Panic fluttered through me. I'd rarely been ill as a child, and this was my first ever visit to the ER.

"Hush. It'll be fine. And when you wake up, I'll be here, okay?" Matt's voice was unbelievably soft. His hand stroked my forehead. "And I'm gonna stay here until they come to get you."

"Promise?"

I heard the smile in his voice. "Promise."

THE FIRST thing I was aware of was my dry throat. Then I slowly opened my eyes, and God, the lights were bright.

"Sarah, he's awake." That was my dad. I blinked in the direction of his voice, and there he was, his face hovering a few feet from mine. "Hey, son. Welcome back."

I tried to swallow, but it felt like the inside of my mouth was coated with sandpaper.

"Here." Dad slipped his hand under my head and lifted me carefully before a paper cup touched my lips. "Ice chips. Don't take too many, all right? Just enough to get rid of the dryness."

Another hand gently caressed my forehead. "Hey, baby." Mom gazed at me, her eyes focused on mine. She smiled. "Was the thought of my leftovers so bad that you had to get put into the hospital to avoid them?"

I snickered. "At least you know now that it wasn't your cooking that got me here."

She laughed quietly, but I saw the shadows under her eyes. It had to be the early hours of the morning.

Then something occurred to me. "Matt? Is he here?"

Dad chuckled. "He's gone in search of a coffee machine. He wanted to be sure to stay awake until you came around." He swallowed. "He did really well to get you to the ER so fast. Unfortunately your condition was worse than they initially thought. Your appendix had ruptured when they finally got you opened up."

I sighed. "Matt the hero. That sounds about right."

"Who's a hero?"

I lifted my head to stare at the foot of my bed. Matt stood there, carrying a cardboard tray with three cups. I smiled. "Where's mine?"

He laughed. "You get yours when you get out of here. You'll be in the hospital for about two or three days, that's all. Then you're coming home, and I get to play nurse." He winked. "I've already been online to find my costume."

If laughter really was the best medicine, I was going to do just fine as long as Matt was around.

NOTE

I'D ALWAYS known that Matt could be relied upon in a crisis. Not that we'd ever had a crisis, you understand, but the knowledge was there somehow, innate but there. That Christmas Day, I found out just how right I was. Matt was a rock.

Of course, in the days that followed, I was to learn just how much of a rock he truly was.

Chapter Seventeen

December 30, 2013

I WAS sick to death of feeling like crap.

You remember I said how I was rarely ill as a kid? Well, seems like that was bullshit. My mom said I was The Worst Patient whenever I had something wrong with me. And after those first couple of days once I'd left the hospital, I guess Matt was ready to agree with her, 100 percent.

I need to go back a bit. After two days of intravenous antibiotics, they discharged me from the hospital, and boy, was I glad. Only thing was, the day I was due to leave, I wasn't feeling so hot. Not that I was about to tell *them* that—I just wanted out of there. Besides, they gave me oral antibiotics to continue to take at home, so I figured it wouldn't be long before I felt a whole lot better.

Mom wanted me to go stay with her, but I didn't want her fussing. I just wanted to be in my own bed, the rest of the world kept at bay by our front door. So Matt brought me home, and those first two days he took care of me, cooking for me, making sure I was drinking plenty of water and taking my meds. When the next day arrived, he asked me if I was okay.

I should have guessed he'd see straight through me. So I did what I had to do—I lied through my teeth. I knew he'd only worry and take me back to the hospital, and no *way* was I gonna have that. But when he had to go into work for a morning, I seized my opportunity. I called a cab and hightailed it to the nearest clinic.

I can hear you, y'know. You're thinking it should have gone to the ER, right?

Wrong. They knew I'd just had surgery. And in my befuddled brain, I told myself that how I was feeling had nothing to do with the surgery. To be honest? It felt for all the world like I was getting a cold, and no way was I gonna go to the ER with a stupid cold.

At the clinic I told them I was feeling generally unwell and that there was something going around at work. They took my temperature, which was 100, and when they asked if I had any recent medical history—I lied. I said no. I said I'd woken up that morning with a "sudden fever" and aches and pains.

Yeah, yeah, I know, it was stupid, but I really didn't want another stay in the hospital. Besides, it looked like my fears were groundless when they did a flu swab and then started talking about some kind of virus. I was handed meds to treat my symptoms and sent on my way.

See? Flu. I was right. I caught another cab home and stumbled into bed, where I think I passed out.

When I came to, Matt was shaking me roughly by the arm. "David? David!" He sounded different, like I was hearing him from the bottom of the swimming pool.

"Huh? Whass up?" Christ, getting my mouth to form words was a chore. "An' why're you yellin'?"

"I kept calling your name, but you were totally out of it. Your sheets are soaked, and you're burning up with a fever."

"S'all right, iss flu."

Matt's eyes bulged. "Since when did you become a doctor?"

I weakly raised my hand. "Saw a doctor… earlier… at the clinic. Got meds."

I watched him scan the box of tablets next to the bed. Instead of appearing pleased that I'd gone and done something about it, Matt gave out a low growl at the back of his throat. "Flu. As if."

"Hurts." I whispered the word, as if saying it any louder would somehow anger the gods who would rain down their wrath on my sorry ass. I covered my belly with my hands. "Here."

Matt stared at me. "Dude, do you know what TSTL means?"

I shook my head.

Matt's glower achieved almost mom levels. "It means too stupid to live. Which, right now? Suits you perfectly."

Whatever else he'd been about to say was lost when I passed out.

I CAN recall very little that happened before I finally came around and was able to make sense of what was going on. I knew I was back in the ER. I caught a few words here and there, and while some made sense, others did not: "severe sepsis," "50 palp," "tachycardia," and high fever. To be honest, everything merged into one big blur, where I felt like I was burning up and my belly was hot. Then everything fuzzed out, only this time it was the drugs doing it.

NOISES. ELECTRICAL humming. Murmurs.

I opened my eyes slowly, blinking at the light above my bed.

"Hey." Matt's soft whisper came from nearby.

"Baby?" My mom, her voice cracking. A hand curled around mine.

I swallowed, but my throat was dry.

"Here." Ice chips to my lips, then blessed coolness. "That better?"

"Yeah." It came out like a croak.

"You don't need to talk, okay?" Then her face was there, in my line of sight. Jeez. My mom looked awful. Her skin was pale, and there were bags under her eyes.

I blinked. "Mom? You... okay?" God, that hurt.

"Hush, now." She cradled my head, and more ice chips slipped between my parted lips. "All you need to know is that you're going to be okay." Then she lowered me carefully back down to the pillow, and I was dismayed to see tears glisten in her eyes. She wiped them away harshly. "Don't you worry about me. I'm not going anywhere."

I tried to assess my physical state. God, I felt... weak. "How long...?"

It was all she'd let me get out. "You've been in the hospital for a week. You're in the ICU."

Okay, even in my befuddled state, that didn't make any sense. I'd have known if I'd been there that long.

Then Matt appeared at the other side of the bed. "Hey. Have you finished scaring us all?" He gave me a half smile. Christ, he looked nearly as bad as Mom.

I began to join the mental dots. "How bad...?"

Matt swallowed hard. "Bad enough that we've been praying for you for days."

"We?"

Mom's hand tightened around mine. "Your teachers at Van Hise, who told all the children about you. The people who work at the bookstore." Her lips narrowed. "And if you hadn't been such an idiot in the first place, we wouldn't all have been scared to death!"

"Why the hell didn't you tell me how bad things—"

Mom cut Matt off with a wave of her hand. "Matt, you can say your piece later when I'm done, but I've been rehearsing this in my mind all the while he was out of it, and as much as I love you, I practiced this to be a solo performance, not a duet."

Her words and the tone in which she uttered them told me one thing at least: I wasn't about to die, not if she was winding herself up to give me hell, because believe me, I knew that tone of voice. Matt's expression as he snapped his mouth shut was almost comical.

"I know you don't recollect any of what's happened to you—the nurse said that's because of the drugs they gave you—but you have been in a god-awful state. David Stephen Lennon, they had to put you in a *coma* so you could get better, and if you *ever* put me through something like this ever again, so help me God, I swear I'll...." She faltered, then bent low to kiss my cheek. "I love you, sweetheart, and I do not *ever* want to be that close to losing you again. Do you hear me?"

I nodded. "I hear ya, Mom."

She smiled. "And now I'm going to call your dad and tell him you're awake." She caressed my cheek. "Don't worry. I'll tell him to go easy on you. I've already torn you off a strip." Another kiss, this time to my forehead, and she was gone.

"Your dad's only in the cafeteria," Matt informed me. "Sarah told him to go eat something, and I don't think he had the strength to argue." He held up a paper cup. "Want some more ice chips? They said your throat would be sore for a while, so if this helps...."

"Thanks." I tried to lift my head from the pillow, but Matt placed his hand on my shoulder and gently but firmly pushed me back.

"Let me." He slipped his hand beneath my head and lifted me with such care that my throat tightened. Then he brought the cup to my lips, and I took some more chips before he lowered me back.

I wanted to ask him about the past week, but at that moment, the door opened and my dad entered. I figured my questions would wait, because it didn't look like I'd be going anywhere just then.

THE HOSPITAL seemed a lot quieter, and I was glad of it. My head was still buzzing from earlier. Mom and Dad had finally gone home. Mom had been reluctant to leave, and my dad had muttered something about "Let me take care of *you* now." That had done the trick.

Matt had stayed, however.

I waited until the nurse had left the room before I started with the questions.

"Was it really that bad?"

Matt regarded me in silence for a moment, and then he came and sat on the bed. "I'm not gonna go into a lot of it, because although you might tell me you're feeling a little better, I'm assured you won't take in much of what's said to you. So let me put this into perspective. You are in the ICU. This is fucking serious."

God, the look in his eyes…. My heart quaked.

"Do you remember telling me your belly hurt?"

I nodded.

"There was a reason for that. The wound from your op was hot and red. You had an infection that had gotten into your system when your appendix ruptured." He took a deep breath. "You wanna know why your mom looks like shit? And me too, probably? That's because none of us has gotten much sleep. Christ, David. There were tubes and lines all over the place, and some heavy-duty antibiotics. More meds to keep your blood pressure up so your heart wouldn't stop." Another calming breath. "David, people *die* from sepsis, and you fucking looked me in the eye and lied to me. And that lying almost cost you your life."

"Matt, I—"

He forced out a long breath. "I stood by your bedside, looking at you lying there, intubated, on a respirator, and do you wanna know what was going through my head? I was so angry, not only at you, but at myself. I knew there was something wrong that day you came out of the hospital, and yet I listened to you and not my own instincts."

"I'm sorry," I whispered. It was only just sinking in. I'd almost died through being a stubborn asshole.

Matt took my hand in his. "I wasn't ready to lose my best friend, all right? And now you're gonna have to put up with me, because I'm gonna be stuck to you like glue until you're on your feet."

"But… you have work…."

Matt smiled. "Yeah, true, but what's the point of being some hotshot business analyst if I can't work from home? And I'm gonna be home until you can take care of yourself." He speared me with an intense gaze. "Now, if your condition remains stable, they'll move you out of here and into a regular room, so you are *not* gonna do anything to jeopardize that, right?" He narrowed his gaze. "By the way… that clinic you visited? They called and left a message. They wanted to tell you that the flu swab came back negative, but that if you were still sick, you should see your doctor right away." He snorted. "I guess that part got taken care of."

"Are you still pissed at me?"

Matt regarded me steadily, his jaw set. Then his face softened. "No, I'm not. I should be, because God knows you put me through it this last week. Now I'm more relieved than anything. But as God is my witness, you do *anything* to set back your recovery, you try this shit again, and I will kick your ass."

I clasped his hand tightly. "I'll be the perfect patient, I promise."

Matt stared at me for a moment, his eyes wide. Then he laughed. "I guess you must be feeling better, because if you can lie like *that* and be convincing… I'm just glad your mom's not here."

"Why?"

"She'd be laughing so hard at what you just said that she'd probably rupture something." He smiled. "Now get some sleep. I'll still be here when you wake up."

"Promise? Pinky swear?" I held up my hand.

Matt chuckled. "God, you're such a kid." He brought his hand to mine, and we hooked our pinkies. "There. Pinky swear. Happy now?"

I sighed, feeling the tension slip from me. "Yeah." I closed my eyes and let go.

I AWOKE with a start, my sheet damp with sweat, the nightmare still clinging to me. My heart pounded. It took a moment to recall where I was.

"Shh, easy." Matt sounded half-asleep.

Wait. Matt?

"Why're you here?"

Matt came into view, rubbing his eyes. "I didn't want to go home. I'd intended on waiting until you were asleep before I snuck out, only I must've been more tired than I thought. I fell asleep in the chair."

Talk about heaping coals.... "Go home, Matt. You've done enough."

He smiled. "Tell you what. I'll wait until you're fast asleep again, and then I'll go. How's that?"

It was clear to me he wasn't going to budge. "Okay."

Matt regarded me closely. "Do you need anything? Some water?"

I nodded, and he poured water into a plastic cup, then put a straw into it. "Okay, little sips, the nurse said."

I drank eagerly, relishing the cool liquid. When I was done, I sank back with a sigh. "Still feel weak."

"You will for a while. And they won't let you out of here until you're stronger. Especially with your track record." He bit his lip.

I knew that look. "What?"

"When I brought you here, I... sort of ratted you out."

"Huh?"

"I was waiting for your parents to arrive, and the nurses kept asking questions, so I... answered them. Which *might* mean I told them how you didn't tell us how you were really feeling when they discharged you, not to mention you lying to the clinic."

I feigned innocence. "How do you know I lied?"

Matt rolled his eyes. "Dude, if they'd known you'd just had surgery, there is no way on this planet that they would've let you walk out of that clinic. So I figured you didn't tell them."

I didn't have a leg to stand on, and he knew it, the bastard. "Back to you ratting me out."

"Well, because you lied to both the hospital and the clinic, you've lost all credibility. They're gonna keep you here until they're convinced you're well on the road to recovery." He gave a shrug. "Sorry, but you only have yourself to blame for this." Then he grinned. "So now you know why I'll be watching you like a hawk for a while."

Under the circumstances, I didn't mind, because the alternatives didn't bear thinking about.

NOTE

UNLESS YOU'VE been in the same position, you have no idea how I felt.
Staring death in the face was kinda… liberating. Literally. Because if it hadn't been for that experience, I might never have found the courage to step way outside my comfort zone and into unknown territory later when I really needed it.

Chapter Eighteen

February, 2014

WHEN I was first moved into a regular room, I naïvely thought that was it. I was going to stay another week in the hospital, and then I'd be back at work.

Yeah, yeah, I know. I was an idiot. I had no real idea of just how sick I'd been or how serious sepsis was. I got a clue, however, when the doctors told me how lucky I'd been not to have developed organ failure or tissue damage.

(One of the first things I did when I got home was to type "sepsis" into a search engine. Yeah. *That* was a sobering moment, I can tell you.)

But that was also the time when Matt went above and beyond. I mean, he was just amazing.

In the hospital they got me moving around, slowly at first, but building me back up to the point where I could take care of myself with such mundane tasks as washing and going to the bathroom. That last one was high on my list, because, people, having to use a bedpan? Not even gonna go there.

So yeah, when they said I could leave, I thought I was fine. The fact sheet that both Mom and Matt took away with them should have told me something.

Mom did her "I want you to come stay with us for a while" thing, but I persuaded her that what I really wanted was for my life to get back to normal as soon as possible. I got the feeling that wouldn't happen if she took me under her wing.

Matt, on the other hand, wouldn't wrap me up in cotton wool. After what I'd seen in the hospital, I had the feeling that a new Matt had emerged, one who wasn't about to take any shit from me. Maybe that was just what I needed.

That first week back home, I remember mainly feeling tired and weak. Food didn't taste quite right. I ached sometimes, and I had difficulty sleeping. Matt, of course, wasn't about to let me dissolve in a pity party. He all but wrestled me into the shower and made me go to bed when I was tired. He kept me moving too, even if it was only walking around the apartment.

But there was less clinical stuff too. Like the meals he made for me, stuff he knew I liked. (Hey, my cooking skills must've finally rubbed off on him!) Back rubs when I ached. Reading to me at night when I couldn't fall asleep. He'd reach for my copy of *Dune*, letting me drift off into a land of magic and spice worms.

Matt had taken a week's vacation to take care of me, and after that, he worked from home as often as he could, so I was rarely alone. Him being there was probably a good thing, because early on there were moments when all I wanted was to be left alone. Moments where I was angry with myself for being so fucking stupid. Moments when I was plagued with insecurity, depression, and a severe lack of motivation. Fortunately those moments were rare, and they passed quickly, mainly because Matt chased them out the door the minute he spied one of them.

After two weeks of recuperation, and still on the antibiotics, I went back to the doctor's to get clearance to go back to work. When they agreed, I really felt like my life was going to return to normal.

Little did I know.

Over the next few months, we got into a routine, Matt and I. He took on more of the cooking, only it was more of him bringing home takeout from one of my favorite restaurants or cafes. The back rubs became part of my week, and along with them came foot rubs too. He'd meet me at the bookstore and walk home with me. Saturday became our day for lazy brunches and strolls around the lake. Friday nights were our movie-and-popcorn times. I couldn't keep track of all the countless ways in which Matt showed how much he cared for me.

I'm not sure when the thought first occurred to me. It wasn't some huge epiphany, more like a little niggling realization that wouldn't leave me alone. I mean, I knew I cared for Matt. Hell, he was like the brother I never had. But it was about that time that a tiny voice in my head quietly pointed out that I loved him.

Not a "he's my brother and I love him" kinda love.

No, this was something different. This was a "I think I've fallen in love with Matt" kinda love.

My first reaction? I shoved that thought away. I knew who I was. I was David Lennon, and I was straight. I wasn't in love with a man. That was stupid. That was preposterous.

Only, that little thought wouldn't stay away.

It kept creeping back into my mind whenever Matt did something sweet or did something that made me smile. And those times when it was just me in the apartment, when Matt was working late, or shopping, or visiting his parents, that was when the thought would sneak back in.

I had to do something, because it was driving me crazy. And in the end, I did the most sensible thing I could think of.

"WHERE'S MATT?" Mom asked as she handed me a cup of coffee.

"He's visiting his folks."

"Mm-hmm." Mom leaned against the kitchen sink and regarded me steadily in that way of hers, the one that always made me think she could read my mind.

"Where's Dad?" I didn't want to talk about Matt. Not just then, at any rate.

"Where else would he be on a Saturday morning than at the Home Depot?"

In spite of my nerves, I had to smile. "What have you got him doing now?"

"Me?" Mom opened her eyes wide. "I have no idea what you mean."

I snorted. "Then let me refresh your memory. First there was the summer house you had him build when I was five or six. Then there was the pond, not to mention the little wooden bridge over it. The deck for your garden chairs. The pergola for your lilacs and jasmine. The—"

"Okay, okay, you made your point, smartass. Now why don't you tell me why you're here? Because I'm pretty certain it's not to discuss your dad's DIY skills."

That was my mom. Right to the heart of the matter.

I studied my coffee cup. "Mom, when I was growing up… did you ever think I might be… gay?" When she said nothing, I glanced up.

She blinked. Then her face softened. "This is about Matt, isn't it?"

I guess it didn't take a genius to figure that part, right?

Before I could say another word, she came over and sat facing me. "Neither your dad nor I ever wanted to presume you were one way or another. And as for Matt…. We figured the two of you would be together forever, however the dynamic worked out."

"Dynamic?" I frowned.

She smiled. "Honey, I watched you both grow up. I've… observed things."

"Like what?"

"Just little things. Like when you used to sit on the couch together, one of you would have his hand resting on the other's thigh. I don't think you even realized you were doing it. And things like Matt's hair."

Now she'd lost me. "What about his hair?"

There was that smile again. "Matt would get a haircut, and every time you walked past him sitting down, you used to rub the back of his head. Then it got so that he kept it short. It was kind of cute. What made it even more cute was seeing him do the same thing with you." She regarded me calmly. "Things just added up. The lack of what I'd call serious girlfriends. The casual affection you shared. The change in dynamic as you grew up. And we weren't the only ones who noticed. Daniel and Maryann saw it too."

Oh God. "You've discussed this with Matt's parents?"

Mom laughed. "Sweetheart, why do you think we've become such good friends with them? We worked out a long time ago that whatever happened, you and Matt were going to remain close, and that meant we would too."

I was filled with confusion. "But Mom… I mean, I'm not attracted to men."

She bit her lip. "From what I've seen, you're not all that attracted to women either. So maybe it's not about being attracted to men or women. Maybe it's about just being attracted to Matt."

I thought about that. "I'd always assumed I was straight."

Mom leveled a look at me. "And what makes you think life is that static? Do you think you're handed a map the minute you're born, and that you have to stick to it rigidly? Life doesn't work like that. *People* don't work like that. And right now, you're just working out that David Lennon's life—and sexuality—is not something etched in stone, but written in the sand." She reached across the table and took my hand. "Everything will be all right, baby. I promise."

I loved her confidence. I just wasn't sure I shared it. Because I wasn't the only one in this equation, was I?

Then I reasoned that the only thing to do was to talk to Matt.

I had to know, one way or another.

I WAS sitting on the couch when Matt came home. There was an open book in my lap, but I wasn't reading—the thoughts in my head wouldn't stay still long enough for that.

He put down his keys on the table near the door and walked over to where I sat. "Hey." He rubbed the back of my head before heading toward the kitchen. "Gonna put together something for lunch."

It took a moment for his actions to sink in, and I couldn't help but remember my mom's words. But... it couldn't mean what she *thought* it meant, could it? Because any way I looked at it, Matt's gesture spoke of... intimacy.

Was I brave enough to say something?

I got up from the couch and walked into the kitchen area. Matt was slicing chicken and tomatoes and chopping lettuce, all the fixings for sandwiches spread out in front of him. He looked over at me and smiled. "You hungry? It won't be long." Then he went back to his task.

That smile....

Then I knew. This was the moment to tell him I loved him.

Yes, it was crazy. Yes, I was terrified. But I wasn't the same David, was I? *This* David had stared death in the face. *This* David had faced the possibility that everything he'd ever known about himself might not really be true.

So I opened my mouth, and nothing came out.

I tried again. Nothing.

My heart pounded, and all the hairs on the back of my neck stood on end.

For God's sake, say something.

"Matt?"

He looked up, and something of my emotions must have shown in my face because he stilled. "You okay?"

I took a deep breath and stepped off the precipice. "I think I'm in love with you."

Matt's eyes widened and his lips parted, but no sound came forth.

Shit. I forged ahead, because that was all I could do now. "I know, it doesn't make sense. But I've never felt this way about anyone my entire life, so I figured… this had to be love. And if it is, then… I'm in love with you."

Matt regarded me in silence, and panic fluttered in my belly with every second that passed. Then after what seemed like an eternity, he cleared his throat. "Do… do you think about me when I'm not here?"

I nodded, incapable of making a sound right then.

"Does it make you feel good when you know you're going to see me?"

Another nod, only now my heartbeat had sped up.

"Do you look forward to the times when it's just us?"

That was when I dared to hope. "Yes."

Matt nodded slowly. "Then… I think I'm in love with you too."

"You… you do?" God, the relief that poured through me in a flood. It wasn't just me.

Matt's eyes clouded over. "You know when I fully realized what love meant? When you lay there in that hospital, and I didn't know if you were going to live or die. All I could do was pray to God that I would get the chance to tell you how I felt. Not that I was sure *what* I was feeling. I just felt so damned helpless, and my stupid heart was breaking because I'd never said those three little words to a living soul, and if I was going to say them to anyone, it would be you." He took a breath. "And here you are. Here *we* are." His face broke into one of those smiles of his, the ones that always brightened my day.

Only, now I knew why they did that.

"This is nuts, isn't it?"

I chuckled, feeling braver than ever. "Who ever said being in love was sane?"

That made him laugh. "So, what do we do now?"

I gestured to the knife he held. "You finish lunch, we eat it, then we play things by ear. Because I don't have a clue, any more than you do."

Matt gave a mock gasp. "David Lennon doesn't have all the answers? Oh my."

"Hush, you. Neither of us knows what we're doing, but we'll figure it out."

He smiled. "We've got time."

That was true. Our current road map was suddenly out of date, and we had no clue where we were going, but we'd figure it out.

Of that I had no doubt.

"And in case you missed it...."

I snapped out of my introspection and found Matt regarding me, those blue eyes filled with warmth. I smiled. "Missed what?"

Matt didn't break eye contact. "I love you."

Hearing those words had me sending up silent, grateful prayers that I'd lived to hear them from Matt's lips. "Love you too." And as usual I covered my nervousness with humor. "Now finish our lunch."

Matt shook his head. "Still a bossy shit, I see. See? The song got it wrong. Love *doesn't* change everything." He went on slicing, but I could see his smile.

I HAD no idea what time it was, just knew it was late and my brain was showing no sign of wanting to shut down. I lay on my back, staring as the lights of passing cars played over the ceiling.

I'd actually said it. I'd stepped out into the unknown, faced my fear, and... Matt was still there. Better—Matt loved me. Matt fucking *loved* me.

I didn't know what I'd expected to happen after such a huge declaration, but the evening had been... quiet. We'd sat on the couch, watching a movie, a bowl of popcorn in Matt's lap. Only now his hand was in mine, his head was against my shoulder, and God, it felt... right. Natural. Like he was always meant to be there. At some point, he'd turned his head to look at me, and all I wanted to do was kiss him.

Why didn't I? Hell if I know. I was playing this by ear, and for some reason I was nervous. Funny thing was, I sorta got the impression he was feeling the same way. The "It's not just me, then" thought was comforting.

"You're still awake." Matt's voice crept across the room from his bed.

"How did you know?"

He chuckled. "How many years have we shared a room?" A moment's silence. "What are you thinking?"

"That everything has changed, and yet it hasn't."

"What do you mean?"

I tried my best to frame my conclusions. "I've always loved you like a brother, y'know."

"Yeah, I know." His voice was soft. "And ditto."

"So today wasn't so much about realizing that I loved you, but more that the way I loved you had changed." It was the closest I got to expressing my feelings.

There was a pause, and I wondered briefly if he'd fallen asleep.

"I wanted to say something when you came around in the hospital, but it wasn't the right moment." Matt sighed. "And then it never seemed to be the right moment, mostly because I was scared how you'd react."

A fear I understood all too well.

Part of me was yelling that he was too damn far away, and then something stirred in my memory. "Do you remember when we went camping by the lake?"

"Of course."

"And we'd share a tent, you in your sleeping bag, me in mine?"

"Where are you going with this?" I heard the amusement in his voice.

"Y'know, I've only just thought about this, but… every night we'd turn out the light before sleep, you on your side of the tent, me on the other. And yet by morning, we'd wake up next to each other. Somehow in the night, we'd… migrated across the groundsheet and ended curled up together."

"I remember."

"What just struck me was that not once did it feel strange. Neither of us questioned it at the time. Neither of us was embarrassed. I wonder why that was."

"Maybe part of us knew, even then," Matt suggested.

My heart hammered as I sat up and threw back the comforter. "My bed is more comfortable than a sleeping bag, and there's plenty of room if you want to join me." I took a quick breath. "Because I'd love to fall asleep with you curled up around me." I waited, my heartbeat racing.

A rustle of cotton and Matt was there beside my bed, dressed only in his white boxers. "I would love that," he whispered. Then he climbed into the bed and I covered him with the comforter. I could feel the warmth from his body, and then my heart soared when he slipped his arm around my waist and snuggled up to me.

Matt... in my bed. His breaths, growing more even, warm on my back. His hand against my belly, a comforting weight.

For the first time in my life, I shared my bed with another person, and what made it perfect was the fact that it was Matt.

NOTE

No... I have nothing to add. This was just... perfect.

Chapter Nineteen

"MATT."

"Hmm?"

"Matt, it's ten o'clock."

"So?" He snuggled closer, if that were even possible. I had to admit, waking up with him wrapped around me was wonderful. I was warm and cozy, his body was firm and—

Holy shit. One part of his body was *very* firm.

"I like this." Matt sounded sleepy and content.

"Huh?" Okay, so I was distracted. I'd asked him into my bed because the thought of sleeping with him seemed right. I hadn't even thought about... sex.

But you can bet I was thinking about it now. And yeah, it was really distracting, because there were like a million thoughts all zipping through my brain at once.

Does he want us to have sex?

What if there's no chemistry? Been there, done that, and the idea that we might not click physically was one I had to acknowledge. I mean, just because right then there was a very hard dick pressed against my briefs-encased ass did not mean a thing. Morning wood, anyone?

I don't have condoms.

Lube! Shit, I just ran out of lube.

And that set my mind off on a whole new trail. I'd heard Matt jerking off a hundred times, and he'd probably heard me too. We weren't the kind of guys who sat on a couch together, watching porn and pulling on our cocks. No, I'd always thought that was private stuff. I mean, I tried my best not to make much noise, but come on, it had to be obvious what I was doing, right? And I figured it was the same with Matt. So did this mean I'd get to watch him? He'd watch me?

God, this was all new territory, and it was scary as fuck.

"Okay, where are you?" A sleepy chuckle tickled my ear. "Because I can hear something really loud in this bed, and I think it's your brain working overtime."

Like I was going to tell him what I was really thinking about.

"We've got lunch with my parents, remember?"

Matt laughed softly, and then he was stroking my belly, gentle and unhurried. "That's hours away. And besides, I don't want to get out of this bed just yet. Not when there's something important we need to do first."

Yup, my heart was racing. "Yeah?"

Matt shifted away from me and pushed me onto my back. He leaned over, smiling. "Good morning." Before I could reply, his lips were on mine, soft as anything, and there you had it. Matt Thompson was kissing me.

I didn't hesitate. I reached up to cup his head and returned his kiss. What made it perfect? It wasn't a "growl in the throat, God I want you" kiss, but a "hey there, it's me" kinda kiss. Our lips brushed, mouths closed, my hands on the back of his head and neck, his hand on my chest, and I lost myself in the sweetest kiss I'd ever known.

Then Matt slid his hand lower, over my nipples, my belly, down the little trail of hair that pointed the way to my—

Oh God.

His eyes met mine. "Can I?"

Shit, that was so sweet. "You don't have to ask." The words came out as a croak.

Matt grinned. "My momma brought me up to ask first." He traced the outline of my cock with his finger, and it twitched at his light touch. "So… these briefs…. They're kinda in the way."

I swallowed. "Then take 'em off."

Matt's eyes darkened a little. He pushed back the comforter and then knelt up on the mattress beside me to slowly pull down my briefs. My dick sprang free, and his eyes widened.

I hazarded a guess. "First time up-close-and-personal with a guy's cock?"

"That would be a yes." He gave himself a shake and finished his task of removing my briefs. As he dropped them to the floor, I cleared my throat.

"Don't I get to see you too?" Because, God, I wanted to.

Matt's face flushed, and he hooked his thumbs under the waistband of his white boxers and eased them down to reveal his slim but rigid shaft. I'd seen a few dicks in the locker room and the showers, but until that moment, I'd never once considered that a dick could be pretty.

Matt had the prettiest cock, and all I wanted to do was touch it, caress it, kiss it….

When we were both naked, he knelt there, gazing at me, until I couldn't stand it any longer. I opened my arms. "Come here."

Apparently that was the right thing to say, because a moment later, my arms were full of Matt—warm, firm Matt—his skin mostly smooth with a faint dusting of hair across his chest, and his legs long, slim and slightly fuzzy. I held him close to me, loving the feel of him.

"Kiss me again," I murmured.

The happy sigh that escaped Matt's lips told me my instincts were good. I kissed him like I'd been waiting my whole life to do it, to feel so connected to another person. And when he broke the kiss to murmur against my lips, I sighed too.

"Want to taste you."

What followed was… wonderful.

I wanted to slow down time, to etch each moment indelibly into my memory. I wanted to remember the feel of soft lips around my shaft, a hot tongue lapping at the head. The gentle touch of his hands as he stroked and caressed me so tenderly. And I never wanted to forget that heart-stopping moment when he locked gazes with me, just before he took me as deep as he could….

Even if it did result in a coughing fit.

Matt sat up, his eyes watering, seemingly mortified, and I couldn't let him think he'd failed in some way. I tugged him to sit astride me, and then I wrapped my hand around my now-aching dick. I looked up at Matt, hoping to show him how much he'd aroused me.

"Do you know how gorgeous you look right now?" I panted, my climax drawing closer with every stroke of my hand on my cock. "How amazing it felt to have your mouth on me?"

His breathing hitched, and he licked his palm and began to work his own hard shaft. "Loved sucking you off." He arched his back and rocked, sliding his dick through his fist. "Never thought it would be so hot."

I stroked his thigh, aware of the tingling throughout my body, the heat that was building inside me, spreading through me in a slow tide. "God, look at you." He looked… breathtaking, his short dark hair spiked up, his lips parted, his belly taut. It was like I was seeing him for the first time, and it felt right that we were sharing this, separate yet connected, both of us edging closer to orgasm.

Matt leaned forward and took my lips in a harsh kiss, and when his tongue demanded entry, I opened for him, my desire for him growing by the second. When he came, his warm come spattering my belly, I groaned at the feel of it. It wasn't long before I joined him, our bodies coated with the evidence of our mutual pleasure.

Matt dropped onto his back next to me and let out a long whoosh of air. "Wow." I started laughing, and he jerked his head in my direction. "You're not thinking about my lack of oral skills, are you?" His face tightened a little.

That sobered me up. "God, no," I assured him instantly. "I was just thinking that a minute ago, I was actually worried that we might not have any chemistry."

He stared at me for a moment, and then he laughed. "You know, I think of you as a smart man, and then you go and say something like that." His eyes sparkled.

My gaze drifted over our sticky torsos. "I think a shower is called for."

"On one condition."

I glanced across at him and raised my eyebrows. "There are conditions?" I grinned. "Is this what I've gotten myself in for? You getting all bossy and making conditions?"

Matt speared me with a look. "I was *going* to say, that when we're done, and we've both brushed our teeth, we have to get back into bed, because I'm not leaving this apartment until we've had a lot more kissing." He gave me a sweet smile. "But I *might* have changed my mind."

I pointed toward the bathroom. "Shower. Now. And don't take too long."

Matt laughed as he swung his legs over the side of the bed and got up. "And he calls *me* bossy." I watched him stroll naked out of the room, noticing for the first time that he had the perfect little ass, firm and tight, with a slight jiggle to it as he walked.

It made me wonder if I'd ever truly seen him before. Then I reasoned that at least I was seeing him now.

I PULLED the car onto the driveway and switched off the engine. Matt had been quiet during the short trip over to my parents' house, and yeah, that bothered me. "What's up?"

Matt turned his head to look at me. "Right now it feels like I'm on a teeter-totter, you know? One minute I'm up in the air, ecstatic about this whole situation, excited, my emotions all over the place, and the next? I get thoughts like, are we moving too fast, what will Darren say, what will my parents say…." He sighed. "And then I have moments where I know that just like being on a teeter-totter, we'll find our equilibrium and everything will work out just fine."

I reached over and took his hand. "One, I wouldn't worry too much about your parents. I don't think we're gonna tell them anything they don't already know. Two, Darren won't say jack shit. He's always been careful to keep his opinions out of your parents' hearing, so I doubt he'll mouth off if they're in the vicinity. And never mind them—Gail would have his balls if she heard him. And three?" I leaned over and kissed him lightly on the mouth. "You're right. Everything will work out just fine." I smiled against his lips.

Matt smiled too. "I'm gonna keep saying this until you're tired of hearing it, but…." He drew back and looked me in the eye. "I love you."

I sighed and kissed his forehead. "Never gonna tire of that, just so you know. I may even record you saying it so I can take out my phone and hear you whenever I need to." I inclined my head toward the cream-colored house. "Ready for this?"

He nodded, and we got out of the car. As we stood in front of the door, I leaned over and whispered, "I love you too." Matt's face glowed.

I dug into my pocket for the key, but Matt caught hold of my other arm. "Wait a sec." He took my hand in his, lacing our fingers. "*Now* I'm ready."

Before I could use my key, the door swung open and my dad stood there, a cup in one hand. "I *thought* I heard your car." He glanced down and stilled at the sight of our joined hands. When he looked up, his face was one huge smile. "And that just made my day. Get in here, you two."

We stepped into the hallway, and Dad called out in the direction of the kitchen. "Sarah? We got any champagne in the house?"

Oh.... Wow.

"Champagne? What in the world do you want champagne for?" The kitchen door swung open, and Mom came into the hallway. I knew the second she saw our hands, because her eyes shone and she brought her hand to her mouth. Then she grabbed the keys to my dad's truck and threw them at him. "Trixie's Liquor on East Washington Avenue is open."

Apparently that was all the instruction my dad needed.

"Back in a while," he said, putting his cup on the table and then pulling his jacket from its hook. He paused at the doorway and smiled at us, and then he was gone.

Mom tilted her head to one side and peered at Matt. "You *did* know your parents are joining us for lunch, didn't you?"

Judging by his smothered gasp, I guess that was a negative.

I chuckled. "Looks like we're having a joint family celebration, then."

Mom nodded fervently and left us. "I'd better text your father to bring more bottles."

Yup. Definitely a celebration.

NOTE

TO BE honest, that lunch was sort of an anticlimax. Oh, don't get me wrong. Having our parents stand with glasses of champagne, toasting our future... that was wonderful. It was just that I'd expected to feel... more.

Let me see if I can explain.

We'd just discovered that over the course of eighteen years, our feelings for each other had undergone a transformation. No, wait. That's not the word. Our feelings had evolved over time. Childhood best friends became more like brothers, and then something amazing happened. Those feelings continued to grow deeper than I would have thought possible. It explained so much about why I couldn't connect with anyone I ever dated. That connection already existed, just not one I fully recognized at the time.

We'd always loved each other, but we'd finally come to see that brotherly affection blossom into a deep-rooted, balls to bones, abiding love. That was quite the revelation—for us.

For our parents? To hear them talk, they'd known for years and had been waiting for us to catch on.

See what I mean? So we weren't confronted with exclamations of surprise or shock, but joy, sheer joy that we'd finally gotten onto the same page. And that joy sort of permeated the whole day, seeping into every look and conversation, every touch and caress. I held Matt's hand a lot throughout lunch, mainly because I was trying to hold on to the fact that it was real. And no one batted an eyelid. Matt's sister wasn't there, but I couldn't see her disapproving—that would have required effort on her part, and I doubted she had the energy. (Was I ever that sloth-like when I was eighteen?)

We still had Darren's reaction to come, but we weren't concerned. We'd have Gail in our corner.

Of course, there were a couple of surprises that Sunday, and they were all from my dad.

Parents… just when you think you know them….

"DAVID, YOU got a minute?"

"Sure, Dad." Matt was in the living room with his parents and my mom, talking about the latest news: Darren and Gail had called to say Gail was pregnant, and they were delighted. I was about to ask who wanted something to drink.

"Come on into the den so we can have a talk."

I chuckled as I followed him into the pine-lined room that had always been his hideaway. "Sounds intriguing. As long as you're not gonna give me The Talk," I joked. When Dad closed the door behind us and gave me a startled but guilty glance, I stilled. "Oh my God, you *are*."

Point to note here. My parents never discussed sex with me. Ever.

I'm not kidding. One day after my sixteenth birthday, I'd discovered a leaflet about safe sex, along with a packet of condoms, in my nightstand drawer. The lack of note, or any subsequent reference to those items, gave me a loud and clear message: this is all you get.

So to find myself at the age of twenty-four, about to embark on a relationship with a guy….

What on earth was my dad about to share?

Dad pointed to one of the two leather armchairs, then sat in the other. "Right. Not really sure how to begin this, but…."

I was dying to let him off the hook, for both our sakes. "Look, Dad, honest, we don't have to talk about this, y'know." What I wanted so badly to say was "Don't talk about this!"

He ignored me, pulled open a deep drawer, and removed a battered-looking paperback, its cover held together in several places with tape. He held it out to me, and I… blinked.

"*The Joy of Sex?*" I couldn't help smiling. "Where did you get this, a garage sale?" It had definitely seen better days.

He chuckled. "Your grandpa gave that to me when I was sixteen."

I gaped. "Grandpa?" Then it hit me. "This is *your* copy?" Yeah, you *know* what I was thinking, right? I wanted to ask if I needed to wear gloves to handle it, but I didn't think that remark would go down so well.

He took it back from me and gazed at it fondly. "This proved very useful." Then he coughed. "But let's not talk about that right now."

"No, let's not," I agreed swiftly.

He placed the book back in the drawer. "The thing is, I was going to buy you a copy when you were old enough to… you know."

Now I knew who I got my shyness from when it came to sexual matters.

"But I didn't," he continued. "No real clue why. Maybe because deep down, part of me already knew that you wouldn't get a whole lotta use out of it."

I smirked. There we were, back to that "we knew way before you guys did" scenario.

"When I got home yesterday, your mom told me you'd stopped by, and she also told me you two talked. Well, when I heard what you talked about, I... went shopping."

Okay, my mind was boggling at that point.

Dad opened another drawer and pulled out a plastic bag. "This is for you."

My stomach clenched at the sight of the familiar bag. "You went to my bookstore?"

Dad chuckled. "Well, it's not actually *your* bookstore, but I get what you're saying. Yes, they were very helpful."

Oh God. With much trepidation, I opened the bag and removed a copy of....

"*The Joy of Gay Sex*?" Then it struck me. "Dad... we don't sell this."

"I know! Well, that is, I found out when I asked if they could recommend a book on the subject." He shrugged. "I just stuck it in a bag your mom had in the drawer."

Oh God. "You asked my coworkers... for a book on gay sex. Did... did you say who it was for?" I was starting to eye Monday with growing unease.

"I might have. I'm not sure." He shrugged. "I figured you might need it. We can all use a little advice sometime."

The fact that he'd gone out to find this for me was absurdly sweet, even if he had accidentally outed me as bi to the whole bookstore. "I don't know what to say."

"'Thank you' is appropriate on these occasions, so I'm told," he commented dryly.

I put down the book, left my chair, and gave my dad a hug. "Thank you," I whispered. I sat back and gazed toward the drawer. "Did Mom know you had that?"

Dad snorted. "Are you kidding? I had to fight her for it sometimes. You think it's in that state because of me?" He guffawed.

You know, there are some things a kid does *not* need to know about his parents.

Then a horrible thought struck me. "Dad? You said they were helpful at the bookstore?"

Dad nodded, smiling. "Especially when they recognized me." His smile widened. "Yeah, now that I think about it, I *did* say it was for my son."

Recognized.... Hell no. My parents had been to the bookstore on more than one occasion.

Monday morning at work was sure gonna be interesting.

Chapter Twenty

SOMETHING WAS wrong.

For one thing, there was a light on somewhere in the bedroom. For another, there was a space next to me where there had definitely been a Matt a couple of hours previously. I sat up and glanced over to his bed. He was sitting up, the bedside lamp switched on, and he was reading a book.

I cleared my throat, and he jerked his head up.

"Oh. Hey. I thought you were asleep." For some reason he appeared embarrassed.

"Matt, it's...." I took a peek at the alarm clock. "Three o'clock."

"I know." He sighed. "I couldn't sleep, so I came over here to read a while. I didn't want to disturb you."

That got me thinking. I peered at our room. "Have you thought about how much more room there would be in here if we got rid of one of the beds?" I knew it was a bold move, but I liked the idea of it being our bed.

Matt chuckled. "Three in the morning and you're thinking about moving furniture?"

"You can talk, mister. Wanna tell me what you're reading over there?"

His cheeks flushed. "Oh. It's... that book from your dad."

Oh really? "And did I give you permission to read my book?" I joked.

Matt pulled the open book to his chest. "*Our* book. It says so, right there inside the cover. 'For David *and* Matt.'" He grinned. "Or did you not see that part? Did you go straight to the pictures?"

Damn it, he really did know me too well.

"And while we're on the subject of reading.... How will us having one bed solve the issue of me reading and not disturbing you?"

I coughed. "I wasn't even considering the reading part. I just want us to sleep together every night." Because so far, that had been... bliss.

160

"Aw." Matt gazed at me, and yeah, that was love I saw in those blue eyes, no question.

"So?" I stared at him. "Read anything interesting that you wanna share with the class?"

He smiled. "Why don't I join you so I can give you my… report?"

I liked the sound of that. "Get your ass over here." I reached out to switch on my lamp.

Laughing, Matt switched off his, scrambled out of bed and across the divide, and then he was next to me, naked and warm. I couldn't get enough of looking at him. Matt was beautiful, and part of me wondered why I'd never noticed that before, because he sure hadn't emerged overnight from a chrysalis or something.

Maybe it was because I was looking at him with new eyes.

"Hey." Matt was regarding me with amusement.

I smiled and lay on my back, holding one arm out in invitation. "Cuddle up and we'll look at it together." Because feeling his body against mine? Seriously addictive.

Matt complied, his head on my chest and the book propped open on my belly.

"So, is it any good?" I asked. I could smell his hair, that apple shampoo he loved so much, and the scent was comforting.

He snorted. "I haven't worked out the plot yet, but there seems to be an awful lot of sex in it."

"Idiot."

"I skimmed through it at first. It has sections on everything you could ever want to know about gay sex—well, everything *I'd* want to know, at any rate."

"Is it very different to having sex with a woman?"

Matt paused for a moment. "Not really, apart from the obvious bit about which part goes where. We still need condoms, but for different reasons. And lube. We're gonna need more lube." He glanced down at our crotches and sucked in a breath. "I'm guessing a *lot* more lube."

I wasn't sure whether I was flattered or terrified.

He yawned, and I closed the book and placed it to one side.

"Not tonight, we don't." I stretched out my hand toward the lamp and plunged the room into semidarkness. Matt snuggled closer, and I covered us with the comforter. God, that felt so good.

A moment later, he broke the pleasant silence that had fallen. "Have you thought a lot about it?"

"It?" I knew what he meant, but I could never resist teasing him.

"You know… having sex."

I presumed he meant with him, but it stirred something inside my head. "I'll be honest, I'm curious. I mean, I haven't really thought sex was that big a deal so far."

He fell silent. "Wow. I thought it was just me."

I knew what I was hoping. We were a good fit—not all that difficult when you consider how long we'd known each other, how long we'd lived together in one form or another. And part of me was hoping that we'd prove to be a good fit in bed.

Because anything else would just be wrong.

Another yawn made me smile. "But no more talking. We have to get up for work in a couple of hours. We can talk about this another time."

"Mm-hmm." Matt was already falling asleep.

I lay there in the darkness, Matt wrapped up in my arms, and considered the change of direction my life had just taken in the space of one weekend.

I felt like the luckiest son of a bitch on the planet.

As I opened the front door to the apartment, I paused and sniffed the air. Lasagna? Garlic? "Hey, you're home early!"

Matt appeared in the kitchen doorway, smiling. "Uh-huh. I worked from home this afternoon. Thought I'd make us dinner."

"Wow. Did you cook, or is it takeout?"

He flicked me with the tea towel he held. "Bastard. I *can* follow a recipe, you know." Then he grinned. "But yeah, it's takeout from Olive Garden."

I laughed. "Go on, what have you got us?"

"That alfredo chicken dip you like so much, with grilled chicken flatbread and fried mozzarella, to start with."

I swear I was drooling. "Oh man."

"Then it's their classic lasagna. And finally…." He paused dramatically.

"Oh, say you did. Say you ordered my all-time favorite dessert and I will love you forever."

Matt gave me an innocent look. "Would that be the black tie mousse cake?"

I dropped my jacket and shopping bag onto the floor and grabbed him, enveloping him in a tight hug. "Okay, what did I do to deserve this? Or is it more a case of what I have to do in payment?"

Matt's breathing caught. "Now there's an idea…."

His mouth was right there, and I couldn't resist. I closed the gap between us and kissed him, softly at first, but then I sought his tongue with my own, and suddenly I had Matt pressed up against the wall and we were kissing like there was no tomorrow. His hands were in my hair, mine cupped his face, and I didn't want it to end.

When we broke apart, both of us breathless, Matt let out a long whistle. "Man. Do I get that every time you come home from now on?"

I chuckled. "Sounds like a plan to me." Then my heart melted when he took hold of my hand and led me into the kitchen.

"How was work?"

I groaned. "I'm gonna kill Dad when I see him. You have no idea how many looks I got today. Seems like everyone was smiling at me."

"Since when is smiling a bad thing?"

I sighed. "When you just know they're looking at you and thinking, 'Oh wow. He's bi?'"

Matt snickered. "After the way our parents took the news, they were probably looking at you and thinking, 'And he's only just worked this out *now*?'"

Yeah, I laughed, because he'd nailed it.

"Now for *my* news." Matt paused, his eyes bright. "I had a call today."

"From?"

"Darren."

I'd known it wouldn't be long before he got to hear about us. "And what was his reaction?"

Matt snorted, and what came out was uncannily like Darren. "Dude! I fucking *knew* it!"

I laughed. "Well, he sorta knew it. You're not gay, for one thing." It had surprised me that no one at the bookstore had mentioned it. Then I figured once they'd gotten used to the idea, *then* the questions would come. And the comments.

"He did say one thing that made me choke up a little."

"Oh?"

Matt nodded. "He said he couldn't think of a better guy to come out for."

Wow. I shook my head. "You have to hand it to Gail. She's worked miracles."

Matt gave another snort. "When you consider the material she got to work with? Hell yes." Then he grinned. "I guess it's official. You and Darren are kinda related. You just got yourself the brother you always wanted."

I walked over to where he stood beside the countertop and put my arms around his waist. "I have you. That's the important part."

Matt looked into my eyes. "You do." There was a husky quality to his voice that was doing things to my insides, something I definitely wasn't accustomed to. A shiver trickled down my spine.

Matt must have noticed something, because he stepped back and out of the circle of my arms. "Okay. Dinner."

I cleared my throat, which had suddenly thickened. "Dinner."

Something was in the air, and I was excited and nervous, all at the same time.

DINNER WAS over, the dishes were loaded into the dishwasher, and I was supremely comfortable. I was stretched out on the couch, with Matt tucked in beside me and a couple of glasses of wine within reach on the coffee table. Neither of us appeared to feel the need to talk, but kisses were pretty high on the agenda. It was as if we were trying to catch up on all the kisses we'd missed.

"If I'd known you were this good a kisser all those years ago," Matt murmured, "camping might have been even more fun."

"I wouldn't change any of those times," I said firmly. "They're some of my happiest memories."

"Yeah, you're right." Matt craned his neck to look directly at me. "But now we get to make a whole new lot of memories." When he casually slid his hand under my sweater and stroked my belly, I couldn't suppress my shiver. He gazed at me intently. "Does that feel bad?"

I shook my head. "On the contrary. Feels really good." His light touch was making all the muscles in my abs dance beneath his fingertips.

"Great." And with that, Matt slid off the couch and knelt beside it, pulled up my sweater, and leaned over to kiss me there.

You know it didn't stop there, right?

One minute we were making out in the living room, and the next we'd fumbled our way into our bed, losing clothes along with way. But once we were there, beneath the comforter, sharing our warmth, then everything sorta slowed down.

Perfect.

Touching Matt was sublime. Stroking his body, kissing where my fingers had laid a trail, getting to listen to the noises he made, noises that told me so much—what pleased him, what aroused him…. God, it was like we were worshiping each other, feeding our souls on the pleasure it gave us.

When we reached the point where we wanted more, I had to laugh when it turned out we'd both been shopping for condoms and lube. Great minds, huh?

And that's when things got really serious. Because we're talking fingers, *slick* fingers going where *nothing* had ever gone before. Mind-blowing discoveries, like "What the hell did you just do?" and "For God's sake, do it again, and again, and again." Moments that almost stopped my heart, like when he looked me in the eyes and told me he wanted to see my face while I was inside him.

Inside him. Sweet Jesus Christ, I was *inside* him, and it was tight, and hot, and so, so good.

Oh my God. Slow rocking into him, feeling him tighten around me.

His legs wrapped around my waist, heels digging into the swell of my ass as he urged me to go deeper.

That feeling of being connected, the one that nearly broke me, when I was as deep inside him as it was possible to be and his arms were around me. I swear my soul wept to see that look in his eyes. The look that said "I love you," and "I'm yours," and "You're a part of me now."

Because I was. God help me, I so was.

And when we came—not together, but that was just fine, because I got to see his orgasm, see him break beneath me like a wave on the shore, before it was my turn to shatter—we held each other and kissed, slow, drugging kisses that would probably have continued long into the night if we hadn't felt the need to clean up. Because... hello? Sticky!

It wasn't some perfect love scene. Fingers went too far, too fast, and yeah, there was the odd "ouch." But God, it was fun, it was hot, it was sexy... and I wanted to do it all over again. And judging by the smile on Matt's face? Yeah, we were on the same page. I knew exactly what I wanted to try next, because the way he looked when I was inside him?

Yeah. Wanted to feel that too.

I had a feeling our book was gonna end up in a similar state to my parents'.

"NOW I know what the book meant about afterglow," Matt murmured into the pillow.

I kissed his shoulder. "You glowing?" I chuckled against his back.

He sighed and twisted his head in my direction for a kiss. "Toasty," he said, before our lips connected. Then he pushed back against me, and I held him, my arm across his chest. "Now I know why I didn't get that much of a rush from sex all these years."

"What conclusion did you arrive at?"

Another sigh. "I was doing it all wrong. And I was using the wrong manual."

I laughed softly and buried my face in his neck. "It was supposed to be me, that's why." I kissed down his back, loving how he shivered. "And now it's gonna be just me, just us."

"I like the sound of that." I knew from the dreamy quality to his voice that he was falling asleep, so I curved my body around his and held him as sleep overtook us.

NOTE

NOT GONNA talk about the sex. Nope. That's between him and me. All you need to know is we have plenty of chemistry, thank you very much. And looking back, I can say it got better. And better.

Chapter Twenty-One

I SORT of floated through that first week of being "David and Matt, the couple." Not that much had changed. We got on with life, like we always did, but now there was an extra richness to our days—and nights. For one thing, I discovered I had a new addiction.

Kissing Matt.

Whenever either of us got home, that was the first thing on the agenda, a kind of "God, it's good to see you again" kiss. Then there were the evenings on the couch, sometimes with clothes, usually without, while we made out like teenagers. I suppose we were making up for lost time.

Not that *everything* was sweetness and light.

Matt came home Thursday and informed me that he'd told his coworkers about us. I got the impression that not everyone had been enthusiastic, but hell, I'd have been surprised if they had been. I mean, come *on*. There are always gonna be haters, right? Seventeen or so years since poor Thomas had been bullied back in elementary school and an amazing change of direction on the political front later, and we still had discrimination, abuse, and violence. I'd like to think that will change, but you know what? I think it will always be with us. There's something in mankind's genes that fears what is different and hates what it doesn't understand.

Okay, off the soapbox....

I took one look at Matt's expression, saw the hurt he was trying desperately to hide, and in that moment I decided I wanted to do something—*anything*—to put back that smile of his, the one that always made me feel good inside. And when the idea came to me, it was *my* turn to hide my emotions, because I was buzzing with anticipation.

I waited until dinner was over before laying the groundwork. "Hey, what about eating out Saturday night?"

Matt arched his eyebrows. "Any particular reason?"

I did my best to make my shrug as casual as possible. "It just occurred to me that we haven't done that since I came out of the hospital."

"True." He smiled. "Where were you thinking of, Dotty's?"

"Maybe," I lied. "We can decide on the night, right?"

Matt nodded. "Sounds good. Now how about we watch TV so I can put this day behind me?" It was the closest he'd get to voicing his emotions.

"Sure. And seeing as I'm feeling generous, you get to choose what we watch."

I totally expected the cushion that came sailing in my direction.

"YOU'RE UP to something."

I gazed at Matt with as innocent an expression as I could muster. "I have no idea what you're talking about." I pulled out of Olive Garden's parking lot and onto the road.

"Bullshit," he said pleasantly. "That makes three restaurants we've visited, and three times you've come up with a reason not to eat there." He arched one eyebrow. "Either they were too busy, or they'd changed the menu, or some other half-assed excuse."

I headed the car south on 151, saying nothing. As we approached East Washington Avenue, Matt pointed to the left. "There's that Korean BBQ place someone at work was telling me about. We could try there."

"I'm not in the mood for Korean." We crossed the intersection.

"Not in the—how can you not be in the mood for something you've never tried?" When I didn't reply, he huffed. "Okay, let's go the tried-and-tested route. Hey, we could go to the Old Fashioned for brats and cheese. Or there's always the Tornado Steak House. I know how much you like your meat."

I didn't have to look at him to know he was grinning.

I ignored his suggestions and turned right onto North Butler Street. "Hey, look, a parking space." I pulled over in front of the plain brick building with its blue-and-white awnings overhanging large windows. I switched off the engine and beamed at him. "That was lucky."

Matt peered through the window and smiled. "Aw. It's a great idea, but really? Naples 15 on a Saturday night?"

I sighed heavily. "Yeah, I know. But we might get lucky." It was one of our favorite places, but you had to book a table because of its popularity. We got out of the car, Matt peering through the windows of the restaurant. It did look packed.

We stepped into the warm interior, and just like we always did, both of us sniffed the air, perfectly synchronized. Then we caught ourselves doing it and chuckled.

At the podium, Nina smiled at us. "Hey, guys. Your table is all ready for you."

"Our table?" The note of surprise in Matt's voice only served to send a ripple of anticipation through me. He grabbed hold of my arm. "When did you book us a table?"

"Oh, a couple of days ago," I said, keeping my tone light. We followed Nina through the crowded restaurant toward a single empty table, draped with a white tablecloth.

I guessed it was what was on the table that made Matt catch his breath.

A slim vase stood on one side, and in it was a single red rose. An ice bucket, complete with a bottle of champagne, stood on the other side, and candles glowed in the center.

He came to a dead stop and stared at the table. "Oh. Oh wow."

I stood beside him and leaned in to whisper, "Welcome to our first date."

Whatever else Matt had intended saying was lost as Salvatore came bounding over to our table, his usual smile in place. "*Buena sera.*" His gaze met mine. "Everything is as you requested?"

I gave him the thumbs-up. "Perfect, thank you." When his gaze flickered over to Matt, I couldn't help smiling. "And this is my date."

I had to give it to Salvatore, he caught on fast. His reaction was not what I'd expected, however. His smile didn't dim at all. "I am thinking this is… new?"

Matt found his voice. "Yes… and no."

I chuckled at that. Then I pulled out a chair for him, and he sat down, apparently in a daze. When I took the chair facing him, I rested my chin on my steepled fingers. "Was it the right choice?"

Matt's face glowed. "The perfect choice."

Salvatore opened the champagne, and once he'd poured us both a glass, he beat a retreat.

Matt regarded the table, the candlelight catching in his eyes. "Okay, one, you're a sneaky bastard. Two, I forgive you for being a sneaky bastard, because three... this is awesome." His eyes met mine. "Thank you. I never expected this." His gaze alighted on the rose. "Really? I would never have thought of you as the romantic type."

I reached across the table for his hand, not caring who saw me. "That's because I've never been in love, until now."

It's amazing how champagne, roses, and candlelight can change a mood. Because Matt was right, of course. I'm not the romantic type, never was. He usually had to drag me kicking and screaming to the movies if there was anything even resembling a chick flick on. But sitting there, seeing the way the candles lit up his face, the way he looked at me as we drank champagne, ate the most amazing chateaubriand filet mignon, and fed each other mouthfuls of Baba...

It was magical. It was wonderful. It was Romance with a capital *R*. And I loved every second of it.

When the coffee arrived, I sighed.

"What's wrong?" Matt's brow furrowed.

"Oh, nothing bad. It's just that I really didn't want this evening to come to an end." I knew that every time we returned to Naples 15, I would recall this wonderful night. My first real date with the man I loved. I doubted anything could top the way I was feeling.

"Who says the evening is over?" Matt gazed at me steadily and licked his lips.

That was all it took for my heart to go into overdrive. Because in that moment I knew exactly how I wanted this perfect night to end.

"Maybe the only way to top a first date is with... another first." I held my breath, waiting for him to catch on.

He didn't let me down. Within seconds he was signaling for the check, and my heartbeat was racing.

I CAN recall very little of the ride home.

What I can recall is the slow, tantalizing way Matt undressed me, before undressing himself.

Him taking my hand and leading me to our bed.

What felt like hours of kisses and caresses, as we let our desire take us over.

Gentle exploration with fingers and tongue, until I was begging him to take me.

And Oh My God, when he finally did…

I looked up into his eyes while he leisurely moved in and out of my body, our foreheads touching, our breath mingling. I wanted to hold on to every precious second, to burn them into my memory so that I never lost the wonder of it all.

Of course, it couldn't last, not at that pace. Languid desire gave way to urgent need, and soon we were crying out, and there was heat, and passion, and subsequent bliss that pulsed through me, *crawled* through me, spreading to every part of my body.

When it was over and my heart was beating normally again, we held each other under the covers, limbs entwined as we kissed. After a few minutes, I rolled onto my back and stared at the ceiling.

"What are you thinking about?" Matt snuggled up against me, his head on my chest, my favorite position.

"If that was what happened after our first date, I can't wait to go on our second."

He chuckled and then stretched, hooking his leg over mine. "I could get used to this." He peered at me. "Think you could cope with making love every night? Because this is seriously addictive."

God, it so was. "I'm thinking we need to write to the authors of the *Joy of Gay Sex*. I think you just invented a few new positions." I grinned. "Hey, maybe they'll name one after you."

Matt snorted. "Trust me, that one was in there. Page sixty-nine. Sixty-nine. Get it?"

I kissed the top of his head. "You're a goof."

"And you love me."

It was true. I did.

Matt knew I was teasing. This wasn't a night for adventurous sex—it was a night of discovery. Another moment to put away our fears and doubts and remember that our hearts belonged to one another, just like they had since that day in second grade.

Even if it had taken us all this time to finally realize it.

THIS WAS just the start of our story. We're a work in progress. We evolve from day to day. It isn't all fluffy clouds, rainbows, and unicorns. It isn't all sweetness and light. We've been together two years as a couple, in a relationship that was eighteen years in the making, so we had a pretty good foundation on which to build. Matt was, and always will be, my best friend, but now he's so much more than that. He's the love of my life, my rock, my shelter, my cheerleader, and my most constructive critic. He's there for me every damn day, just like I am for him, and I don't see that changing anytime soon.

I remember him looking at me a lot those first days, like he couldn't believe it was real. He even put it into words once.

"How come we didn't see what was happening?"

I don't have an answer for that. Maybe the timing wasn't right. Maybe it needed that jolt when we both thought I was gonna die to push us into action. Maybe we weren't ready to accept the truth back then.

And what is the truth?

I love Matt. He loves me. End of story.

Except that's never the end, right?

Epilogue

November 30, 2016

I CLOSED the lid of the laptop with a sigh. "Finished."

Matt jerked his head up from his book. "What? *Finished,* finished?"

I had to smile. "Do you know how adorable you are when you repeat words like that?" It was a habit of his. "And yes, finished, finished."

He sat upright, his eyes gleaming. "Well? Word count! We demand a word count! Did you do it?"

I beamed. "Fifty thousand and eleven words."

Matt threw his paperback into the air. "Woo-hoo! You amazing man!" He held out his hand. "Now hand it over."

I blinked. "What?"

"I wanna read it."

I snickered. "I just this minute typed the last word. I haven't even done a read-through. It'll need editing. Tidying up. A shitload of work."

Matt set his jaw. "Don't care about any of that. You've poured your heart and soul into that document for the last thirty days. I wanna read it."

I sighed. Like I could refuse him anything. "Here." I held out the laptop.

"Yay!" He took it and made a dash for the bedroom.

"You're not gonna read it here?"

"Nope!" he yelled back.

Actually, that probably worked out better, because I would have been watching his face the whole time, and that would have bugged the hell out of him.

An hour later, I knocked quietly on the door. "Do you want something to dri—"

"Reading here. Go away."

Wow. "God, you're bossy." I went back into the living room and tried not think about Matt reading my magnum opus. (Yeah, I snickered at that too.)

Another hour passed before I brought up the subject of dinner. Nope. Yet another terse remark that he was still reading. What was he doing, writing a goddamn critique of it?

When he'd been in there for a total of three and a half hours, Matt emerged from the bedroom, his eyes red, his face flushed. He stared at me in silence for a moment, and then he launched himself across the room and into my arms and kissed me with a fervor that held nothing back. I couldn't help but respond. I returned every kiss, matching his passion, caressing his face and neck, kissing his cheeks, lips, and forehead.

When we finally parted, he regarded me with shining eyes. "My God, David. It's beautiful. I love how you wrote us."

I wanted to weep with relief, but I held my emotions in check. "I'm glad you like it."

Matt widened his eyes. "Like it? I fucking *love* it!" He paused, and that was when I knew something was coming. I knew that look.

"I'm waiting for the 'but.'"

He smothered a gasp. "Damn. You really *do* know me, don't you?" He sighed. "Okay. It's the ending. I think it needs to end differently."

"And I suppose you have an idea about that?"

He smiled, one of *those* smiles. "Let me finish it."

"Huh?"

"It's only fair. You've told the story, but it's my story too, so...." His smile widened. "I want to have the last word."

I snorted. "Like you don't always get the last word anyway."

He bit his lip. "Can I? Please?"

I pointed toward the bedroom. "Go on, then."

To my surprise, Matt shook his head. "Not now. When it's right."

"And when will that be?"

He shrugged. "I'll know." He tilted his head. "So, are you gonna publish it?"

That was when it struck me. I hadn't begun the writing with the aim of publishing. It had been solely a means of making a check on the list of things I'd always wanted to accomplish. But now that he mentioned it....

"I suppose I could." Instantly my mind started going over what would be required to bring the manuscript to that point: an editor, a cover, proofreaders....

Matt's face glowed. "I'll buy the first copy. You can sign it, for your number-one fan." His eyes twinkled. "I promise not to go all Kathy Bates on you."

I gave an exaggerated shudder, and he laughed. He was right, of course. The last word should go to Matt.

I couldn't wait to see what he wrote.

June, 2017

HI, EVERYONE. I thought it was about time I introduced myself. I'm Matt.

Thank you for reading our story. I can attest that every word of it is true—well, most of it. Not gonna rat David out for the bits he embellished. But yeah, this is the story of how we met and fell in love.

I chose this moment to add a note because I wanted to share with you how much I love this man. I'm typing this in one of my favorite places in the whole world—down by Lake Mendota, where we're camping out like the little kids we once were. David surprised me when he drove us here, but not half as much as when he took me for a walk down to the water's edge and asked me to marry him.

You know I said yes, right? Hell, my eyes are still leaking.

So I'm gonna leave this right here while I go and spend some time with my best friend and future husband.

And our story isn't over yet. Not by a long shot. Maybe I'll write the sequel—in another twenty years or so....

K.C. Wells started writing in 2012, although the idea of writing a novel had been in her head since she was a child. But after reading that first gay romance in 2009, she was hooked.

She now writes full-time, and the line of men in her head clamoring to tell their story is getting longer and longer. If the frequent visits by plot bunnies are anything to go by, that's not about to change anytime soon.

K.C. loves to hear from readers.

Email: k.c.wells@btinternet.com
Facebook: www.facebook.com/KCWellsWorld
Blog: kcwellsworld.blogspot.co.uk
Twitter: @K_C_Wells
Website: www.kcwellsworld.com

BEFORE YOU BREAK

SECRETS

K.C. WELLS & PARKER WILLIAMS

Six years ago Ellis walked into his first briefing as the newest member of London's Specialist Firearms unit. He was partnered with Wayne and they became fast friends. When Wayne begins to notice changes—Ellis's erratic temper, the effects of sleep deprivation—he knows he has to act before Ellis reaches his breaking point. He invites Ellis to the opening of the new BDSM club, Secrets, where Wayne has a membership. His purpose? He wants Ellis to glimpse the lifestyle before Wayne approaches him with a proposition. He wants to take Ellis in hand, to control his life because he wants his friend back, and he figures this is the only way to do it.

There are a few issues, however. Ellis is straight. Stubborn. And sexy. Wayne knows he has to put his own feelings aside to be what Ellis needs. What surprises the hell out of him is finding out what Ellis actually requires.

www.dreamspinnerpress.com

DEBT
K.C. Wells

Two months after Mitch Jenkins had the rug pulled out from under him when his two-year relationship came to an abrupt end, he is still hurting. A colleague's attempt to cheer him up brings Mitch to a secret "club." Mitch isn't remotely interested in the twinks parading like peacocks, until he spies the young man at the back of the room, nose firmly in a book and oblivious to his surroundings. Now Mitch is interested.

Nikko Kurokawa wants to pay his debt and get the hell out of the Black Lounge. Earning his freedom isn't proving easy, especially when he starts attracting interest. Life becomes that little bit easier to bear when he meets Mitch, who is nothing like the other men who frequent the club. And when Mitch crawls under his skin and into his heart, Nikko figures he can put up with anything. Before long he'll be out of there, and he and Mitch can figure out if they have a future together.

Neither of them counted on those who don't want Nikko to leave....

www.dreamspinnerpress.com

DREAMSPUN DESIRES
OUT OF THE SHADOWS
K.C. Wells
Can he step out of the shadows and into love's light?

Can he step out of the shadows and into love's light?

Eight years ago, Christian Hernandez moved to Jamaica Plain in southern Boston, took refuge in his apartment, and cut himself off from the outside world. And that's how he'd like it to stay.

Josh Wendell has heard his coworkers gossip about the occupant of apartment #1. No one sees the mystery man, and Josh loves a mystery. So when he is hired to refurbish the apartment's kitchen and bathrooms, Josh is eager to discover the truth behind the rumors.

When he comes face-to-face with Christian, Josh understands why Christian hides from prying eyes. As the two men bond, Josh sees past his exterior to the man within, and he likes what he sees. But can Christian find the courage to emerge from the darkness of his lonely existence for the man who has claimed his heart?

www.dreamspinnerpress.com

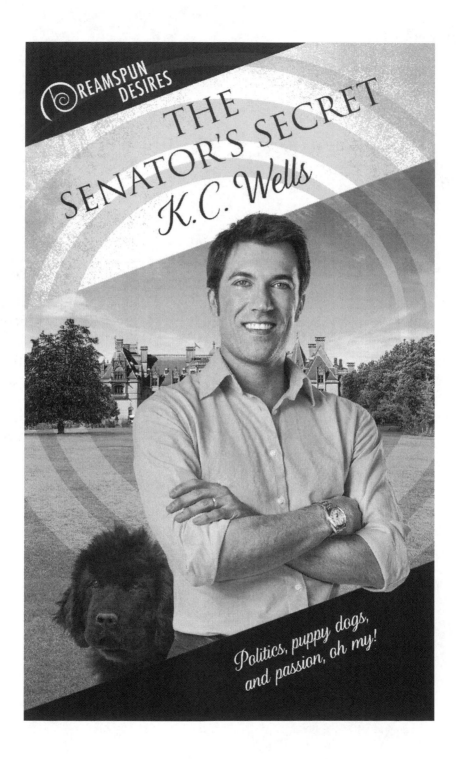

DREAMSPUN DESIRES

THE SENATOR'S SECRET

K.C. Wells

Politics, puppy dogs, and passion, oh my!

Politics, puppy dogs, and passion, oh my!

When his Republican opponent outs him with a photo in a Facebook post, Senator Samuel Dalton doesn't have many options open to him. It doesn't matter that the photo is totally innocent. He has no choice but to come clean… until his staff suggest putting a spin on it that leaves Sam reeling.

Sure, he'll end up with a lot of sympathy, not to mention the possibility of more voters from the LGBT community, but it still seems a pretty drastic solution.

Now all they have to do is persuade Gary, the other man in the photo, to play along. It sounds so easy: convince the constituents of North Carolina that he and Sam are engaged.

No big deal, except for the fact that they've only just met.…

www.dreamspinnerpress.com

Step by Step
K.C. Wells

Jamie's life is one big financial mess, and it really isn't his fault. However, the last thing he expected to find in the library was a Good Samaritan. He might have been suspicious of Guy's motives at first, but it soon becomes apparent that his savior is a good man who has been lucky in life and is looking to pay it forward. Guy being gay is not a problem. Jamie's not interested… or so he thinks.

Guy is happy to help Jamie, and the two men get along fine. But when Jamie's curiosity leads him from one thing to another, Guy finds himself looking at the young man with new eyes. What started out as a hand up is now something completely different….

www.dreamspinnerpress.com

In the kingdom of Teruna, the red-cloaked Seruani teach the Terunans the art of love. Taken from their homes at seventeen to be trained, they are shunned as outcasts by society and considered the lowest of the low. So when Prince Tanish falls in love with the Seruan Feyar, the man who took his virginity and the only one to share his bed, he is not about to declare that love. No one can ever know, because the consequences would be too painful to consider for both of them.

When the king of Vancor visits Teruna, he promises that his son, Prince Sorran, will marry Prince Tanish to solidify the alliance between the two kingdoms, with the proviso that the virginal Sorran is instructed in the art of pleasing his husband-to-be. When Tanish's father chooses Feyar to be this instructor, the lovers decide Prince Sorran must be taught that this is to be a marriage in name only....

A resentful prince, unwilling to share his lover.

A resentful Seruan, unwilling to share his prince.

And the shy prince whose very nature sparks changes in the lives of all those around them.

Teruna is about to change forever.

www.dreamspinnerpress.com

A BOND OF TRUTH

K.C. WELLS

Sequel to A Bond of Three

It is twenty years since the Bond of Three returned to Teruna. The kingdom of Kandor, once Teruna's enemy, seeks help and sends its finest warrior, Dainon, on a diplomatic mission. A solitary man since his wife and child died, Dainon is unable to explain why an encounter with a young man on a beach rocks his world to its core.

Prince Arrio of Teruna has always been attracted to men but has never acted on it—until he meets Dainon. Headstrong Arrio goes after what he wants, despite his fathers' advice. But when Prince Kei arrives unexpectedly, Arrio finds himself drawn to both men. Is history repeating itself?

Prince Kei has his first taste of freedom and is shocked when the visions that have plagued him since childhood become reality. The three men embark on a voyage of discovery. No one has foreseen the day, however, when the arrival of a stranger threatens to destroy their bond.

www.dreamspinnerpress.com